THE HIDDEN GUNMAN

Margaret crossed to the porthole and looked out. A movement across the way at the Nugget Saloon caught her eye. Someone had quickly lifted his head above the false front and then ducked out of sight. It looked like Lobo Lafferty. Swiftly she crossed the room, stood on tiptoe, and grabbed Cap's Winchester. Her whole being prayed that it was loaded. She jacked the lever and saw that it was, then rushed back to the porthole. She aimed at the place where the head had appeared. No need to yell a warning to Dolf if she didn't have to, but if she did, she would yell and shoot both. This time the figure on the roof came up with a rifle and started to take aim. She was quicker, firing off a shot, then jacking in another shell. The rifleman, whom she was now sure had been Lobo, dropped from sight.

She yelled, "Duck, Dolf! There's a man across the street with a rifle!"

Dolf, who had turned toward the sound of her shot, spun around, his long-barreled Colt already in his hand....

MORGETTE AND THE ALASKAN BANDIT

G. G. BOYER

LEISURE BOOKS NEW YORK CITY

A LEISURE BOOK®

June 2002

Published by

Dorchester Publishing Co., Inc.
276 Fifth Avenue
New York, NY 10001

ISBN 0-8439-5027-7

The name "Leisure Books" and the stylized "L" with design are trademarks of Dorchester Publishing Co., Inc.

Printed in the United States of America.

Visit us on the web at www.dorchesterpub.com.

MORGETTE AND THE
ALASKAN BANDIT

PROLOGUE

MARGARET Morgette lovingly watched the tall, lean form sprawled nearby on the screened porch in a big homemade deck chair. Her husband, who was ninety-four that year, didn't look a day over seventy, though the perilous life he'd led would have put a less hardy human into the grave at the half century mark. His hair wasn't even entirely gray, not unusual for a Morgette. Nor did his flesh hang on him, as was the case with most very old men. He still stood straight and, as she knew, one of his greatest pleasures was personally tending by hand their big vegetable and flower garden—which was hard work.

She smiled at the light snoring that issued from under the battered Stetson pulled down to shade his eyes. This nap was an after-breakfast ritual that she hadn't minded at all once she'd figured out that it was good for him. They'd been married fifty-seven years, largely eventful ones. And, although she didn't know it yet, this year would be no exception. They'd spent a great part of those years right there in Alaska. It seemed as much like home to her as anywhere; after all, they'd lived all over the frontier before it had died. That had been due to his inclination, not hers. She guessed that if she had to put a word to his lifelong calling it would have been that of "adventurer."

She was soon to be reminded of one of their most exciting shared adventures—and about to start another—right there on their Yukon River stamping ground. Perhaps it was her well-developed Indian second-sight that was at work as her mind idly drifted back to the first of those adventures. The year had been 1889. They'd just returned from Idaho, her birthplace, and the location of the Morgette ranch—the first in that country. There, four years before, she'd run off and married Dolf Morgette, whom her father, Chief Henry, had told her was a "great warrior." Her father and Dolf's father had been great friends in the days before her people had been driven off their land, crossing the Rockies for a thousand miles to flee the army, eventually whipping the pants off them until they were finally overwhelmed. The tribe had been banished to hot, sticky, and unhealthy Indian Territory for almost a decade and had just returned when Dolf, a fugitive, had landed in their camp seeking a hiding place. He'd been seriously wounded, and she had nursed him back to life. And fallen in love with him. She had known from the first time she'd seen his lean, craggy face with its strong chin and sweeping black mustache, even etched with pain and haggard from his ordeal, that this was no ordinary man. Now he'd become a legend in his own time. Hollywood had even made a movie based on his life. But in those days his people hadn't thought of him as a "great warrior." They called his breed "gunfighters." His people didn't consider him famous—but notorious, or even infamous; he'd been a killer of the breed of Wild Bill Hickok.

Thinking of all this, she looked at him and almost giggled. She thought, some killer. Dolf Morgette, retired gunfighter. He'd been one of the gentlest, most considerate men she'd ever known—when left alone. He didn't even kill rattlesnakes unless they were where some kid might stumble across them by accident. He'd always say, "They're gentlemen; they warn you before they throw down on you."

Margaret herself was far from being the stereotype of an old fat squaw. She was still lean and active, mentally and physically, and apt to fight Dolf over who got to hoe what in the garden. Even before she'd met Dolf she'd had a fair education in the "white man's" schools back East. Over the years she'd greatly improved that start by reading widely and associating with many famous people in the Indian Rights movement—even appearing on the lecture circuit with such as Tibbles and Eastman. In all this Dolf had been entirely supportive. She considered him a most unusual man in many ways. Before she'd met him he'd become a self-taught lawyer, studying while unjustly jailed for five years—railroaded for what had clearly been self-defense. She had good reason to know that he'd broadened that start through his lifelong reading of everything that came to hand, or that he'd ordered or bought in bookstores on the rare occasions they'd been near one.

The sound of bulldozers working the distance reminded her that they had both outlived the pioneer era. The U.S. Army Engineers were putting the final touches on a nearby runway for the Air Corps. Its primary use was intended to be for the ferrying of lend-lease aircraft to the U.S.S.R. She lived today in a different, almost alien, world, one she was not entirely comfortable with. She wished she could accept it as readily as Dolf seemed to. He'd say, "It's all part of living to an old age." Then he'd recall how eagerly Mum, his grandmother, had grasped change, thrilled by any newfangled convenience. Then he'd add, "She came in with Andy Jackson and went out with Teddy Roosevelt. I guess us Morgettes all aim to live as long as we can and enjoy it while we're at it." Actually Mum had lived a trifle longer than he'd said. She had died at 103 and had been buried with her shotgun, just as she'd demanded. At the age of fifteen she'd used the shotgun to fetch an Indian she'd caught trying to steal the colt that Dolf's grandfather had given her as a wedding present. Margaret had never blamed her for the exploit since Margaret had been raised understanding the rules of horse stealing herself.

She had to admit Dolf was certainly growing old and enjoying it. He was almost never sick. She'd signed on with the Morgette destiny in 1885, expecting to look after him till he died, since she was seventeen years younger. She'd often sigh and wonder if she were going to outlast him. She sighed again just then, admitting to herself, "It isn't going to be easy."

Her train of thought was interrupted by the arrival in their circular gravel driveway of a miniature Army motorcade—a jeep followed by a six-by-six truck. Their arrival roused Dolf, who stood up and stretched, then yawned. She always marvelled at how tall he still was—at least six foot two; he'd once been two inches taller.

"What the heck have we got here, Maggie?" he wondered.

Their son, Henry, was in the jeep with two others. He'd been a fighter ace in World War I and had been recalled to active duty after Pearl Harbor. It was hard for Margaret to realize that her son was a colonel now. She watched him jump lithely from the jeep—spry yet at fifty-six. She thought, he's a chip off the old block for sure.

Henry motioned to his parents. "C'mon down here and see what we just dug up," he invited.

Colonel Hancock, the local chief of the Army Engineers, jumped down followed by his driver. He followed Henry around to the rear of the "six-by." The two drivers, both corporals, joined the group after Margaret and Dolf. One let down the tailgate. In the dim, canvas-shrouded interior Margaret could make out a large rectangular box.

"What in the world is that?" she asked.

"I can guess," Henry said, "but I figured you two might know for sure."

Margaret finally deciphered the barely legible lettering, obscured by mud, on the front of the bulky box; she also figured out the meaning of the combination dial and handle on the front. It was a rusty old safe. She felt a thrill of anticipation, suspecting what it probably was.

"We pulled it out of the muskeg over there near the river," Henry explained. "Do either of you know what it is?"

She'd have suspected from the location where it was found, even if the dim lettering "Baker and Hedley" hadn't been recognizable. She remembered the last time she'd seen it—being pulled away from Baker and Hedley's trading post in a wagon. It had been in July of 1889. That was just a few weeks after the ice had gone out of the river. In Old John Hedley's keeping had been a lot of the spring cleanup of placer gold from the Sky Pilot mining district, in which they were then still living.

Dolf looked at the safe, then at Margaret, then nodded at their son. "I reckon we both know what it is, and you, too, as much as you've heard about it. But that's not the big question."

The other army men all realized there was some old secret about to be unraveled here, and they waited eagerly to hear what it was.

Margaret thought she knew what Dolf would say next to amplify his remark, and she was not disappointed.

"The big question is whether the stuff is still in it or not."

"Well, Pa," Henry said, "if it was an inside job like we suspected it might have been, it'll probably be full of old shot sacks. They would have filled it so Old John wouldn't think it was too light and look inside to check."

Dolf nodded. "We'll soon know—if you fellows can get it open."

The mention of an inside job brought a thought to Margaret she'd never dared mention to Dolf—and still wouldn't, knowing how loyal he'd always been to his friends. The thought was, I wonder if that robbery was part of Old John's retirement plan. Well, we'll soon know it wasn't if the gold is still inside. She felt a twinge of guilt. Old John Hedley, for all of his fierce ways and grim independence, had always been like a father to her. But he'd been an old scoundrel, as even Dolf would have admitted. Lovable to his friends, but a highbinder nonetheless.

Margaret clearly recalled the day the safe was hauled away. Precautions had been minimal since no strangers had been seen in the settlement; besides, there was no place to hide the gold if someone got away with it in the first place—or so they had all thought. Old John's store had been prudently located well above the high waterline. (In fact, the ruins of the store were still there.) She could see the store in her mind; the men trundling the heavy safe out on its own wheels across the heavy planks from the platform and into the big wagon, causing the wagon's springs to sag. The team had a job getting the load rolling over the soft ground, they then headed down the hill and around the bend into the willows where the boat dock was located. Suddenly, rapid gunfire had crashed out from that direction.

Dolf had burst into lightning action, grabbing his Winchester which had been leaning against the building and streaking toward the sound. He'd been about to go along as one of the boat guard on the trip downriver. Old John had rushed into the store and back out packing his famous double-barrel Greener, hotly legging it after Dolf. As he'd sprinted off Dolf had yelled back at her, "You stay there!"

She thought now, how like him to be cool even under the stress of such a moment. She grinned inwardly remembering how she'd promptly disregarded his command. She'd dragged young Henry and Maggie inside, turned them over to Elsie Hedley, grabbed a Winchester and a box of cartridges from behind the counter and headed after the men, loading her rifle on the run. She'd never believed very much in leaving her man's safety merely to God's mercy and Dolf's overconfidence. Besides, she'd been told that the Great Spirit was male and, having observed His record of occasional fumbling, concluded He was in need of all the help He could get. He might get overconfident and forgetful. Males were prone to do that, in her opinion.

MORGETTE AND THE ALASKAN BANDIT

CHAPTER 1

"I CAN tell it's your first time North by the way you're dressed," the moon-faced little fat man was telling Dolf Morgette.

The two were standing at the rail of the *Idaho* as it rolled and pitched its way through the Wrangell Narrows.

Margaret Morgette, Dolf's wife, reclining in a deck chair a few feet behind them, almost laughed aloud. She thought, the new gold discoveries up north are attracting all kinds. She wondered how long this cocksure little fellow would last. Some of them did, much to the surprise of the sourdoughs, and were accepted at worth. She doubted this one would be.

"You're pretty tall," the fat man went on, "six-three I'd judge at least. You won't stand up under a back pack like a burly fellow like me."

To herself she said, Fat, not burly; fat is definitely the word. She grinned. She knew Dolf would politely and amiably put up with this bunkum all day if he had to, all the while exposing a bland exterior through the ordeal, and occasionally putting in a word, or grinning, or perhaps nodding his head. She suspected that if the little fellow knew who Dolf was he'd probably get the vapors and fall overboard. The sly notion to let him know tugged at her mind, causing another grin. Dolf would probably give her the devil if she did, but it would be worth it. She resolved to wait her chance.

She looked over her husband's tall form, wondering what the stranger saw that led him to mistake Dolf for a cheechako—a green horn. Anyone familiar with the frontier would have read "curly wolf" all over him. His chin, now in profile, was almost too massive, a family trait revealing his bulldog determination. Of course it was accentuated just then by his even teeth clenched on a cigar. The sweeping black mustache, slightly salt-and-pepper at forty, tended to balance the heavy chin, but emphasized his high cheekbones: high as her own Indian ones. But the florid complexion and deep blue eyes would have dispelled any notion he might be Indian. Most of the time his steady, deep-set eyes were friendly, but she knew they could turn almost black—cold as ice— and assume the fire of a glaring, cornered wolf. He had never looked at her like that, and she was glad he'd never had occasion to. After reflecting on the whole matter, she supposed it must be Dolf's city clothes that threw the fat man off, right down to a nobby pair of russet shoes and a fedora.

When Dolf had bought the outfit in San Francisco, their friend Will Alexander had accompanied them. Dolf had felt it necessary to explain to Will, "I always kinda hankered after a set of dude clothes. Wondered what I'd look like in 'em. Besides, Maggie's been pestering me to get some civilized clothes."

"I have not," she'd protested, and she really hadn't. She'd known he was kidding her, but had risen to the bait anyhow. Privately, she thought he looked best in no clothes at all. When he'd got his new clothes on she'd thought he looked just fine in them too (still did, as a matter of fact)—like a prosperous businessman, which he was in a sense of the word. (A very remote sense of the word.) When they'd returned to the Alexander mansion, however, Will's wife, Clemmy, had almost choked; she'd never seen Dolf in anything but a plain sack suit and his high-heeled boots and wide-brimmed Stetson. "You're not the type, Dolf," was her opinion. Typically, Dolf had only grinned. He was a man who went his own way, even with his friends. Maggie suspected he liked his looks in his new duds, though he was far from vain and would never have admitted such a thing. To

Clemmy he'd replied, "I derned near bought a derby lid too—may yet." He hadn't though. Some drunk in Juneau, which was full of old westerners, might have taken a shot at it if they hadn't recognized him.

Margaret was recalled from this reverie by the fat man's eager remarks. "Don't run off. I wanta show you my new-fangled gold pan." He rolled rapidly away on his short legs—headed for his cabin, no doubt.

Dolf rested an elbow on the railing, took a deep drag on his cigar, and grinned at Maggie.

"We can hide somewhere," she offered, returning the grin.

"I kinda like the little feller," Dolf said.

"You would."

"Be nice to him. He'll learn."

Margaret thought, He sure as heck will if I have anything to do with it. And it won't be long, either.

Dolf mused, "He's not the only tenderfoot on board. We'll probably see a lot more of 'em with the diggin's picking up all over the Yukon Valley."

"I know," Margaret said. She'd been amused by the greenhorns' dress, as unusual for them as Dolf's was for him. But they'd looked a lot less at ease in theirs. The fat man was decked out in a parka (far too warm for November on the Inland Passage), kersey pants, felt boots worn inside of knee-high rubber boots, and a high-crowned fur hat with ear flaps that could be tied under the chin. He'd even bought a pair of fur gauntlets he tied with a string worn behind his neck, like dog team drivers did. He'd already shown Dolf his nickeled .22-caliber pistol which he carried in the side pocket of his parka. He'd confided to Dolf, "Lots of bad men up where you're headed—I'm a crack shot with this thing."

Margaret had thought, "You'd better be. In fact, you'd better hit whoever you shoot with that thing right between the eyes. If you don't you'll make 'em mad enough to wear you out." She wasn't surprised to see that Dolf hadn't even batted an eye over the "crack shot" remark. She'd have bet the little fellow couldn't consistently hit a washtub with his .22 at ten feet. Margaret had seen a lot of shooting in her short life—too much—some good and some bad: mostly the latter. She'd been on the long flight of her tribe in 1877 when they'd fought pursuing army units in several battles. She'd seen soldiers so green they'd obviously never fired their guns. Unfamiliar with their rifles, they shut their eyes in anticipation of the heavy recoil, flinching so badly they ended up hitting only the ground a few feet in front of themselves. She knew that some cowboys who thought they were gunmen were apt to do the same thing. The little blowhard fat man struck her as falling into the same category.

He came hotfooting back in a short while with a sizable cardboard box under his arm. Dolf had taken a seat next to Margaret, and the man pulled up a chair between them. He placed his box carefully on top of it and extracted his contraption. The gold pan was obvious enough. But it was fastened at an angle by a bent metal rod to the top of a pyramidal device perhaps a foot high, and, from the way he hefted it, of substantial weight. He set it on the deck, then fished in the box and extracted a monstrous key which he inserted in a hole in the base and started winding. It seemed to Margaret that he would never be done. When he was, he glanced from Margaret to Dolf like a magician about to extract the proverbial rabbit from a hat. He pushed a lever, stood back with his arms spread and said, "Here goes!"

Nothing happened. "It's supposed to start," he muttered, looking dismayed. He tapped it lightly. Still nothing happened. Maggie, watching Dolf try to keep a straight face, giggled. It netted her a disapproving look from the fat man.

"I'm sorry," she said. "What is it supposed to do?"

"It's a mechanical gold pan. Cost me eighteen bucks in Chicago."

At that Margaret involuntarily guffawed loudly.

The little man impulsively kicked his mechanical marvel,

inspiring it into sudden convulsive action. In a small jiggly storm of motion it walked across the deck before it finally overturned and flopped around like a chicken with its head cut off.

At that Margaret couldn't help but howl; tears started rolling down her cheeks. Dolf tried to give her a reproving look, but couldn't help chuckling himself. The man pursued his machine (which now looked like it was having a fit), grabbed it firmly, and tossed it overboard. He dusted off his hands. By then both Dolf and Margaret were roaring with amusement. He looked from one to the other soberly, grinned a little, then started to laugh as hard as they were.

When they all finally quieted down he said, "I reckon my wife was right. She said I was a derned fool to give eighteen bucks for that thing. It turned over a pot of her pansies in our parlor and scared the cat up on top of the portiers the first time I tried it out. The dog even bit it—and I won't say what else. You can imagine—the night before I left." He looked melancholy and added, "I shouldn't have left it out on the floor in the parlor."

He shook his head. Then his face registered a new thought. The opposite of a poker player's—chubby and guileless, with watery blue eyes—it was an almost instant indicator of his thoughts. His fat lips didn't help, protruding under a dinky, undernourished blond mustache that perched on his top lip like a diver ready to spring off. A receding, lumpy chin was a perfect complement to the rest. Margaret would have bet that he was balding under his cossack chapeau, but she couldn't tell since he'd worn the hat even at meals.

"I haven't even introduced myself," he said apologetically. "I'm Hubert Smith—everyone calls me Hubie. I run Hubie's barber shop in Chicago—got three chairs. I've a brother in Juneau who's a big shot there. That's how I happen to know so much about Alaska. We write regular." He offered a small, fat hand to Dolf, who shook it, being careful not to break it by accident. He was surprised to find the little man's grip a lot stronger than he'd expected.

"Name's Dolf," he said. "This is my wife, Maggie."

"Howdy ma'am." He gallantly doffed his hat and bowed slightly. As she'd expected, he was bald.

"I didn't catch the last name," he said to Dolf.

Margaret, debating whether to grab her chance to reveal who Dolf was, lost it when Dolf quickly said, "Morgan." She wondered if he'd suspected what was on her mind and gave him a sidelong glance, but couldn't tell. They frequently traveled under the name Morgan to forestall the ghoulish curiosity of those who wanted to pump a killer, especially a noted gunfighter. People seemed as fascinated with them as with poisonous reptiles.

"Pleased to meetcha both," Hubie said. He squinted at Dolf. "I figured I knew your face from somewhere, but I guess not. You ain't by any chance an actor, are you?"

"Nope," Dolf said. "In cattle most of my life. Goin' north for my health. Doc's orders. Clean, cold ocean air."

Hubie nodded. Margaret almost laughed. However, she did remember Doc Hennessey seeing Dolf off and saying, "It might be healthier for you to get out of here again. Can never tell when someone'll decide to try evenin' up an old score."

Plenty of them in the Quarter Lien district of Idaho had old scores against Dolf—and Doc too for that matter. A little over a decade ago Dolf and Doc had been leading lights in a range war. It had ended up with Dolf being put in the pen for five years and being nationally famous. He'd only been back on short visits. The last time might have engineered a few more scores if anyone knew who'd left so many bodies decorating ponderosa limbs here and there in out-of-the-way spots. It had put a stop to the wholesale rustling in the district and undoubtedly saved the Morgette ranching interests from showing a loss. Dolf's brother Matt and his son by his first marriage, Junior, ran the ranch—the oldest in the district and one of the largest. Dolf's kind ministrations had also saved a lot of other ranchers from losses—in the case of the less successful ones, perhaps disastrous losses—but she was sure plenty of those would overlook that in order to "tut tut" about that terrible man, Dolf Morgette, at the least excuse.

Hubie talked awhile longer, then said, "I guess I'll turn in for a nap. This ocean air makes me sleepy."

After he was out of sight Margaret heaved a big sigh. "You deserve a medal for being so nice to such people," she said.

"It doesn't hurt anything," he said. "The little guy has a good heart."

"And big mouth," Margaret added.

"Maybe he ain't allowed to gab at home like I am and is getting it out of his system," Dolf kidded.

"Gab? Somedays I don't get two words out of you. I wish you would gab."

Dolf grinned and placed his hand affectionately on her arm. "How'm I doing' today?"

"Great. Keep it up."

"For starters, how come we don't know a Smith in Juneau who's a big shot?"

"Search me," Margaret said. "Maybe he's a half-brother—or, say, how about Goldie Smith?"

"Hardly," Dolf said. Goldie ran the biggest joint in Juneau, with whiskey, women, and cards available at all hours.

It left Maggie's well-developed bump of curiosity unsatisfied. She vowed to find out more about Hubie and his brother at the first opportunity. She was good at making such opportunities. Her first one came at the evening meal. She noticed Hubie casting speculative glances in their direction when he thought they wouldn't notice. They were at Cap Magruder's table as they had been at every meal. The *Idaho* belonged to Baker and Hedley, and the Morgettes were friends of both as well as of the captain. Margaret would have bet that Hubie was wondering who they really were—especially because they were sitting at the Captain's table. She thought, Fair enough. I wonder who you really are, Hubie Smith—and if you're as guileless and inoffensive as you look, or whether that's an act. As many enemies as Dolf had, she was always made nervous by the careless manner in which he allowed strangers to approach him. And, she thought, who's Hubie's big shot brother that we've never heard of? His story "sounded" on that angle. She was sure Dolf thought so too. She set out to do some fancy snooping in her own style.

"Would you like to make someone happy?" she asked Captain Magruder, leaning over and quietly voicing the question so Dolf wouldn't head her off.

Knowing her ways, the captain was a trifle hesitant about leaping in without testing the water with his toe. "Maybe," he said. "How much is it apt to cost me in the long run?"

She grinned. "If it does, I'll pay," she promised. "I can promise you no glassware will get broken if that's what you're worried about."

He chuckled. "What's in it for me?"

"A good laugh."

"You're on: I'm your patsy. What do you need?"

She waited until she was sure that Hubie wasn't looking, then pointed him out to Magruder. "See that little guy over there. We met him this afternoon up on deck. Dolf likes him. I'm betting he'd give a lot to be able to write home to his wife and say he sat at the Captain's table. He's really funny. Let me tell you about this afternoon." She told the captain about the automatic gold pan, which even now was probably still giving a spasmodic kick when the spring reawoke—as springs have a habit of doing before gasping their last—at the bottom of the Wrangell Narrows.

"I wish I'd seen it," Cap said. "I'll send the purser over for him."

Hubie approached shyly, looking as though he were wondering if he should salute the captain. Magruder was the sort who seemed to demand that. He was a regular old salt, perhaps sixty, with heavy overhanging gray eyebrows above a seaman's transparent blue eyes, red-faced, craggy-jawed, and possessed of a truly impressive beard down to about the third vest button. He radiated authority and, like most captains, expected instantaneous responses from his employees—with no guff. Maggie could readily imagine him keelhauling some recalcitrant. He unbent and said to Hubie, "Pull up a chair. I hear you're a friend of the Morgans," he added, being careful to use their assumed names, since he knew why they used them and heartily agreed with the need.

Hubie nervously sat down. He looked first to Margaret, then Dolf. "Howdy again," he said. "Much obliged."

"Hi, Hubie," Margaret said. "I'd like you to meet Captain Magruder. He's an old friend."

Hubie obviously didn't know if he should offer to shake hands. Cap recognized this and offered him his.

"This is a real honor," Hubie managed the grace to say. He was thinking, Wait'll I tell the old lady about this in a letter.

Magruder offered him a good cigar which he readily accepted and lost no time in preparing to light. When he had it ready Dolf struck a match and held it out for him.

"Thanks," Hubie said. In view of his impressed look, Margaret wouldn't have been surprised if he'd added "sir" or kissed Dolf's hand. She noticed the intent look he gave Dolf as though he were about to remember having seen his face on *Leslie's Weekly* or *The Police Gazette*.

Magruder sensed that there was more than philanthropy in Margaret's request to get Hubie over to the table, and suspected she probably wanted to pump him about something. Deciding to help out, he sent the purser for a big whiskey for Hubie. When it came the little fat man eyed it as though he were going to say he never drank. Then his natural appetite overcame his acquired hypocrisy. At home

he was a steady churchgoer and never drank—solely because his wife insisted. She'd also insisted he go join his
brother in Alaska, after reading about the several substantial new gold finds there. Hubie had attended a business
school before he'd become a barber. That had given her an
idea.

"You go," she ordered him. "Your brother's letters say he's
an important businessman in Juneau. Go to work for him,
and then go find gold after you learn where it is."

How the hell do I do that? Hubie asked himself, being
careful not to utter the thought aloud. To her he said, "He's
never asked me to come up."

She retorted, "He's never told you to stay away, either."

Hubie had known he was going to lose the argument. He
always did, but in a rare outburst of rebellion he'd asked, "If
you're so all-fired anxious to get rich—and maybe end up
having someone freeze to death in the bargain— why don't
you go?"

"Because I'm a woman." Actually, she looked more like a
haycock, including—or perhaps especially, her hair. It was
seldom combed. It drove the little barber nuts. The thought
had already tugged around the edges of his consciousness
that she was giving him a golden opportunity to split the
breeze and never bother to find his way back. It was not the
least of the reasons why he gave up that three-chair shop
without a bigger fight.

He'd even had the idea of wooing and winning an Indian
princess. He was, perhaps, confusing Alaska with a South Sea
paradise. Up till then he'd never seen (or smelled) an Indian woman. Eventually he'd do both. After all the hassle at
home he'd had one final argument. "Why do I have to go
with winter coming on?"

She had an answer for that too. "The fare is cheaper. I've
been readin' all about it. Besides, you'll be ready to go up to
the gold district first thing in the spring, ahead of a lot of
others. They say it's just over the hill."And she may, indeed,
have read that it was; probably she had. Hubie didn't know

then, any more than she did, that the gold, other than the Treadwell mine at Juneau, was "just over the hill" about six hundred miles or so. Six hundred miles down the Yukon through a inhospitable country and treacherous waters, with perhaps the biggest hazard being the mosquitos about whom sourdoughs joked, "They carry off eagles and eat 'em." If he'd known that he would have been sure to mention it. Her last words had been, "Maybe you'll discover one of them big gold 'bananas' like they do." It was the best she could do with the word "bonanza." She wouldn't have been one of the brighter ornaments of her public school even if she hadn't needed glasses.

Margaret asked Hubie to tell the others at the table about his fabulous automatic gold pan. Reluctant at first, he warmed up to his work and turned out to be a pretty good storyteller. "Dumbest thing I ever did," he finished, and got a general laugh.

"Hubie's brother is in business in Juneau," Margaret said. "One of the big shots, I guess."

This got the desired result. "What sort of business?" Cap asked.

By then Hubie was on his third whiskey; in any case he was not inclined to dissimulate, sober or not.

"Damn if I know." he said, then put his hand to his mouth. "Par' me ladies, I di'nt mean to cuss."

"It's all right," Margaret assured him. "I know men do." She was thinking, do I ever!

Hubie sensed that Margaret didn't entirely believe that he didn't know what business his brother was in and hastened to reassure her. "Hey, I wasn't kiddin'," he said. "Old Rupert is pretty close about what he does, but I guess it's some kind of big store."

Magruder had been listening. "Rupert Smith? How long's he been in Juneau—must be new?"

"Nope, we been gettin' letters from him from there for at least four years. Moved up from Deadwood."

Magruder shook his head. "There sure ain't no Smith

store. Not in Juneau. There's a lawyer named Smith. And of course, there's Goldie Smith runs the Skookum."

"That's it," Hubie burst out, snapping his fingers. "I can never remember names. Skookum Enterprises was what he wrote to Ma once in a letter."

Everyone at the table played it poker-faced. They suspected that Hubie's family must be pretty strait-laced on the Victorian midwestern pattern. But that didn't alter the fact that the Skookum was the biggest saloon, gambling joint, and whorehouse in Juneau. And as far as the gambling went, the crookedest. Obviously Hubie was going to be in for a big shock. Goldie had also operated over in the Sky Pilot till the law, such as it was, had run him out.

"I see," Magruder said. "Well, it's a big outfit all right. I'm sure your brother'll be glad to see you. Does he know you're due in on the *Idaho*?"

"He doesn't know I'm due in at all. Me and the wife planned it as a surprise."

Dolf, who was quietly following the talk, thought, it'll sure as hell be that all right. I wouldn't miss it for a heap. "When we get into Juneau," he offered, "I'll run you up to the Skookum myself."

"I'd be obliged," Hubie said.

Dolf was as good as his word. He left Margaret to go on up to the hotel a few doors beyond by herself, and steered Hubie onto the front gallery of the Skookum. Hubie eyed the sign. "Hey, this is a saloon," he almost bleated.

Barely grinning, Dolf said, "Sure is. Biggest in town. Biggest in the territory as a matter of fact. C'mon in." He swung through the batwing doors. Goldie himself was standing at the bar. Dolf thought, this couldn't be better. The little owner of the Skookum looked up and noted who had entered. For a moment he was unable to keep the look of displeasure from his face, then he quickly ironed it out and assumed a bland mask.

"Well, well, well. To what do we owe this honor?" he asked Dolf.

"I brought your long-lost brother to town, *Rupert*." He clung snidely to the last word, rubbing it in.

Goldie's mouth dropped open—whether at the news or the use of his name, Dolf couldn't tell. He obviously hadn't seen Hubie for awhile. He said, "Well, I'll be jiggered. Is that you, Ralph?"

"I'm Hubie," Hubie said.

"Oh? Is that you, Hubie?"

"I reckon," the little fat brother said weakly. The last minute had all been too much for him. Remembering that he'd had a good Christian upbringing, he clasped Goldie warmly.

Dolf thought, I wish he'd kissed him. Just then he spotted a welcome familiar face emerging from the back of the bar. He could imagine where it had been and what it had been doing. The stairs to the girls' rooms was back there. Of course, he could have merely been out to the water closet.

"Knucks," Dolf called. "What the hell are you doin' down here? I figured you'd be up at St. John."

Knucks eyed Dolf as though he wasn't too sure Dolf was here, either. He said, "We wasn't expectin' you till spring, if ever. Jeez, are you a sight for sore eyes. And have I ever got a bunch to tell you!"

"Later," Dolf said. "This won't keep." He drew Knucks closer and talked to him in a low voice. "How long you been in town?" he asked.

Knucks looked puzzled, wondering if there was some danger impending. He glanced around warily.

Dolf said, "There's no danger. I got a little scheme I want to work on a new friend. See that little dude I came in with?"

By then Goldie had his brother at the bar a few yards away and was talking to him in low tones.

"Here's what I got in mind. I imagine you know the gals upstairs by now?"

Knucks said, "A few of 'em."

"Good," Dolf said, reserving the thought that the few would run right around one hundred percent of them. In a very low voice he instructed Knucks about what he'd like to do for Hubie.

Knucks guffawed. "Done," he said. Then whispered, "You gonna stay around and watch?"

"Cain't," Dolf said. "Maggie's over at the hotel alone waitin for me. Come on over and tell me how it went—and that other bunch of news too. Supper's on me. Knowin' you I'd say you could probably use some solid food about now."

Knucks left for the back to arrange the reception Dolf had suggested for Hubie.

While Dolf had been talking to Knucks, the two brothers had been engaged in earnest conversation. Dolf could guess what part of it was from the look he got when he waved goodbye to Hubie.

Hubie had mentioned to Goldie that Mr. Morgan, who'd brought him in, had sure been nice to him. Goldie said, "So he gave you that Morgan shit too?" Hubie looked stunned.

"Waddaya mean?" he asked.

"He travels under that name. You know who the hell that is?"

"No."

"That's Dolf Morgette, the meanest son-of-a-bitch with a six-shooter alive." Then he added in a very low voice, "But maybe not for much longer."

Hubie didn't catch the significance of the latter remark at once.

"Jeezuz," he said to Goldie. "You know what I did? I showed him my pistol and told him I was a crack shot. It's a wonder he didn't shoot me when I hauled it out. I'm sure glad I didn't offer him a shooting lesson. The thought entered my mind—he looked so much like some kind of businessman."

Goldie just shook his head. He thought, Little brother, you got a hell of a lot to learn about people's looks.

By then Goldie's remark about Dolf maybe not being alive much longer entered Hubie's consciousness. "What'd you mean about Morgette not bein' around much longer?" he asked.

Goldie eyed his brother speculatively, wondering if he could trust him. He decided not. He wasn't about to tell him about his old grudge against Dolf. Or who had hired the rough crowd. He passed it off with, "There's a rough crowd in town that's got a grudge against him. Been waitin' for him to blow in."

Hubie asked, "How do you know? Shouldn't we tell him?"

Goldie's eyes narrowed slightly. "He can take care of himself. He wouldn't be any more on guard if you told him than he normally is." He hoped that satisfied Hubie. "Just hang around and you may see some history made," Goldie said mysteriously.

Any further conversation along that line was cut off by the first installment of the reception Dolf had thought a nice little guy like Hubie should have.

CHAPTER 2

MARGARET had been prepared, by similar past experiences, for her encounter with a new desk clerk at the hotel. They had stayed there before, but Dolf had always been with her when she'd come in to register. This time only Dolf's big hound Jim Too was with her. She disliked the clerk at first sight—a tall, skinny man with a narrow face and slitted pale blue eyes. She also detested his dishwater-blond hair, which she considered characterless. If that was simply a prejudice she found its match in spades, starting with the evil look the clerk cast first at Jim Too, then her. His lip curled as he said, "We don't put up dogs or klootches." He had obviously mistaken her for a local Indian squaw.

Jim Too, sensing a threat in the man's tone of voice, raised his hackles. Margaret hadn't changed expression at the insult. She knew she could simply say she'd come to pick up the reservation of Mr. and Mrs. Dolf Morgette, but pique prompted her to make it difficult for this lout. Instead, she sat down in one of the lobby chairs, determined to wait for Dolf.

"Lie down, Jim Too," she ordered.

He flopped down protectively at her side, keeping an eye on the clerk.

"I guess you didn't hear me," the clerk said. "I said—"

"I *heard* what you said," Margaret snapped. The man was obviously startled by her excellent English, but wasn't ready to give up yet.

"We don't allow loitering either." He pointed to a "No Loitering" sign over the desk.

She glanced out the lobby's front window to see if Dolf were on his way up. He wasn't, but she spotted Cap Magruder headed that way. She figured that he would soon be at the hotel, so she played her next card.

"I'm not loitering. I'm waiting for my husband."

"Well, wait somewhere else."

He started around the registration desk, obviously intending to hoist her bodily out the door if necessary. To do this he had to enter an alcove, then come out through the door into the lobby. When he was out of sight Margaret dipped her hand into the large granny bag she carried as a purse. Inside she always kept a double action .41 caliber Colt Lightning six-shooter, a fact that Dolf managed to successfully ignore in the interest of domestic tranquility. He knew she could use it properly and wasn't apt to accidentally shoot herself or anyone else.

Margaret felt perfectly calm and not the least bit guilty. Her hand was firmly gripped in the business position around her pistol.

"C'mon! Out!" the clerk said roughly as he approached, motioning with his thumb.

Jim Too rose with a deep-throated roar and barred his way. The clerk stopped and took a step backward. Then another.

"Call that son-of-a-bitch off or I'll shoot him," the clerk cried, fear on his face. He shot back into the alcove and almost dove for the desk. Before he could put his hand on the gun he was obviously after Margaret met him from the front side of the desk with a cocked six-shooter aimed at his gizzard. She did a fair imitation of Dolf as she ordered, "Freeze, Mister."

The look on the mean, narrow face would have made the reputation of a villain in a melodrama. His eyes widened and his mouth opened above a sagging, quivering jaw.

"No," the clerk quailed. "Easy with that thing! Don't you

do it! Aim it a little to one side! You'll hang if you shoot me!"

Margaret only glared at him, not turning as she heard the front door open. "Is that you, Cap?" she asked.

She was relieved to hear Magruder say, "Yep. What the hell's goin' on here?"

Margaret relaxed, very carefully letting down the hammer on the Lightning.

A look of immense relief crossed the clerk's face.

"What happened?" Magruder asked, now beside her.

"He was going to shoot Jim Too among other things."

Cap eyed the clerk evilly. "You don't say? And what other things?"

"He threatened to throw us out."

"Do tell," Magruder said.

To the clerk he commented, "You been drinkin'?"

The clerk knew that Cap was "just like that" with Old John Hedley who owned the hotel. "No sir," he assured him. "Never drink on duty." He was beginning to suspect he'd performed a well-known Alaskan maneuver known as "crapping in your mukluk." He looked at Margaret and wondered who the hell she was.

"I guess I made a mistake," he allowed lamely. "I'm sorry, lady."

Cap eyed him severely. "It's apt to be your last one unless you convince this lady to bail you out. She's Dolf Morgette's wife. That's his dog. If you'd shot him or laid a hand on her they'd be fittin' you for a pine overcoat in the A.M. and measuring out the crepe lining."

The apprehension on the clerk's face was something to see. He looked as though he might be thinking of bolting for the back door.

"Jeez, Mrs. Morgette," he said. "I apologize."

His tongue stuck far into his cheek, Cap said, "If the lady says it's okay I'll hide you down on the *Idaho* till Dolf leaves town—in case he hears what happened. Is that okay, Margaret?"

Maggie, suspecting that a practical joke was imminent,

said, with the proper tone of reluctance, "I don't know."

The clerk pleaded, "Please, Mrs. Morgette. I was only following orders."

"Whose orders?" Cap demanded suspiciously.

"Old John Hedley's," the clerk said.

Cap saw his chance to slip in another needle. "I don't believe that. This lady is John's daughter." He knew the clerk wouldn't know that wasn't so.

"Oh, Christ," bleated the clerk.

"I don't want you killed," Margaret said, "so go ahead, Cap. Hide him out. I'll keep mum."

"Oh, thanks, lady, thanks. I never meant nuthin'. I was only followin' orders, like I said."

"Shut up," Cap said, "and give me a piece of paper and an envelope."

He wrote a note to his mate on the *Idaho*, sealed it, wrote "To Mr. Tullywine" on the outside, and gave it to the trembling man. "Don't open that," he ordered, "or Tullywine may suspect it's phony. Now haul your freight out the back quick and get down to the *Idaho*. I see Dolf headed this way."

The man left at a fast lope.

"What did you put in that note?" Margaret asked.

Cap laughed. He sanitized his version to Margaret, but what he had written was: "Lock this son-of-a-bitch in the brig for a few days, then kick his ass off the *Idaho*."

Margaret grinned. Dolf came in and asked, "Aren't you registered yet?"

"We can't turn up the clerk," Cap said. "He's probably drunk somewhere. I guess we'll have to register ourselves." He went around behind the desk. "I'll play clerk. I've been here often enough."

He winked at Margaret. She thought, my, how little Maggie has grown. A few years before she'd have guiltily crawled outside and waited meekly for Dolf, never telling him what had happened in order to spare him anguish. She'd probably have said she didn't want to go in alone or had stayed to enjoy the air or the scenery.

In their room, at last Dolf told her, "I ran into Knucks Geohagen over at the Skookum. He's bustin' with some kind of news, so he'll be over to spill it. I invited him for supper."

"Good," Margaret said. She liked Knucks, a rough-and-tumble friend of Dolf's from his days in the penitentiary. Both he and Gabriel Dufan, their staunch Métis friend from Montana, had been with Dolf on the Barbary Coast almost two years ago, before accompanying him back to Alaska and the dying frontier.

"Did Hubie find Rupert?" she asked, snidely referring to Goldie's real name. "How did he take finding out what his bigshot brother's mercantile company actually was?"

"Not too bad," Dolf said. "He was a 'leetle' shocked at first, but I was surprised how well he took it—to tell you the truth." He paused, then added, "So I thought I'd have Knucks arrange another little surprise for him—probably for Rupert, too."

"What?" Margaret asked.

"Wait'll Knucks comes over. It'll make a better story if we find out how it worked out."

"Knowing you two, I can hardly wait."

She was busy getting some things out of their steamer trunk which had been delivered shortly after Dolf arrived. The early Arctic darkness had fallen so she was working by lamplight. She'd taken the precaution of pulling down the shades as soon as she lit the lamp. She never said why she insisted on doing that, but Dolf knew: in ground-level rooms, particularly, she feared some old enemy or hired assassin would take a pot shot at him from outside.

She lay down for awhile, missing their young son Henry terribly as she usually did at this hour of the day. It had been their special time to romp together. But at the urging of her father, Chief Henry, she'd agreed to leave him in his village until spring. Dolf had jointed the chief in persuading her that it was a key time for a boy almost four years old to learn the language and ways of her people.

"I miss Henry," she said.

"Me, too," Dolf admitted. "But I think we did the right thing."

"Suppose he catches something and dies?"

"Could as well happen in Alaska."

"But we won't be there if he does."

"Worryin' won't help. We left him and that's that. He'll be up after the ice breaks out." He meant the ice on the Yukon, since by then they'd be up in the interior at St. John in the Sky Pilot district.

"Well," Maggie sighed, "at least Father promised to send for Doc Hennessey if he gets sick."

Dolf wondered if the Chief really would, or whether he'd send for Strong Bull, the tribe's head shaman. He wasn't about to voice that thought to Maggie. And he was far from sure that Strong Bull's hocus-pocus hadn't once saved his own life. One thing was certain: if all went well, his grandmother, Mum, and Doc Hennessey would bring Henry to them in the spring. Doc was finally closing out his practice in Pinebluff—he'd said. "Need a rest," he'd explained. He'd been the district's only doctor for years. Now there were several others since the mines were booming again.

Knuck's rap on the door interrupted Dolf's thoughts. "Who is it?" Maggie asked before opening it.

"Santa Claus," Knucks replied.

"You're early," Dolf said, when she had opened the door.

"For Christmas or supper?"

"Not for supper."

Dolf got up from where he'd been sprawled on the bed and put on his coat. Knucks looked him over critically. "I was aimin' to say somethin' about them fancy duds," he said.

"Say away. But you may end up payin' for your own supper," Dolf warned.

Knucks put on a guileless expression. "I was only goin' to say you looked like a dude."

Maggie laughed. "That's what some tenderfoot on the boat

thought. He even warned Dolf about all the bad men up North."

They went out down the hall.

"You don't say?" Knucks commented. "Well, I can vouch for that. And I guess I saw your tenderfoot over at the Skookum. He had a bit of a 'do' after you left, Dolf."

He saved the details until they were seated in the dining room and had ordered. Dolf had tapped on Cap Magruder's door on their way past, and he'd joined them.

Knucks warmed up to his story with a few flourishes, addressing his implausible introductory lies to Maggie. He said, "Well, young lady, your husband, knowin' I'm a regular churchgoer, figured I might know some of them fallen angels over at the Skookum who come in regular on Sunday to ask the good Lord for indulgence."

"Indulgence for what?" Cap asked.

"Poor singin' voices in the choir, I reckon," Knucks said, looking bland.

"Anyhow, it happened I did know a couple. So, followin' instructions I found someone to show me where I might find them."

"Did you?" Dolf asked.

"Five, to be exact."

Dolf stirred his coffee, poker-faced.

"Well," Knucks continued, "still followin' instructions to the letter you understand, I crossed their palms with a little coin of the realm and hired them for a 'leetle' melodrama. To make a long story longer, Hubie, the tenderfoot, and his brother were still gassin' at the bar when the first one of them gals strolled in and waltzed over to our pigeon and planted a big kiss on him and squealed, 'Hubie! I ain't seen you since Chicago!' I gotta say he took it as well as Goldie did. Hubie pushed her away and said, 'I never laid eyes on you before.' So she looked hurt and said, 'I get it. You don't want anyone to know. I'm sorry.' So she moseyed on over to maybe promote a sucker at the poker tables." He paused like a good storyteller should just about then, having loaded everyone with the information that there were still four angels in reserve.

"What happened then?" Cap asked.

"Would you believe—?"

"Wait a minute," Dolf interrupted. "You said Hubie took this all better than Rupert did. How did Rupert handle it?"

"Who's Rupert?"

"I must've forgot to tell you, Knucks. That's Goldie's front handle."

Knucks guffawed. "Haw, that's rich. I'm gonna pass that all over town. Anyhow, *Rupert* looked like he didn't believe Hubie. Also like he respected him a lot more than he had."

Dolf nodded. "That figures."

"And would you believe them other four traipsed out one at a time and did the same number on Hubie?"

"I would," Dolf said. "I would indeed believe that."

Cap laughed. "I wish I'd seen it."

"I think it was mean," Maggie said. "Hubie seemed like a nice man." To Dolf she said, "I thought you liked Hubie."

"I do," Dolf said. "And I think I'm going to like him even better. How did he handle the other four?"

"He finally caught on to the 'sell.' In fact he told the last one, 'I can't remember your name, but let's go somewhere private to talk over old times.' She was the best lookin' one of the bunch, too."

Dolf said, "Now I know I'm gonna like him even better. I think I'll go over in the A.M. and ask him to give me some shootin' lessons with that shiny .22 of his. I'll bet by now he'd never bat an eye."

Their food came before Knucks could tell them why he'd battled his way over from the inside after snow had started flying in Chilkoot Pass.

He told his story while putting away his chuck. Margaret

thought he put down enough moose stew to keep a small platoon stoked for a few days. Dolf knew Knucks had been on a high lonesome and may not have had a square meal for a week.

"New discovery back of the Sky Pilot," Knucks said. "Looks big. Old John wanted to git the word out before next year."

It figured. Baker and Hedley were out for the gold that could be had over a trader's counter. The more miners and prospectors in the country, the more they stood to make.

"Anyhow," Knucks continued, "the last boat went down the river before the big strike, and the Yukon was way past slush ice then. They're prob'ly froze in somewhere for the winter. Thunder and Lightning came out with me."

The latter were Old John's (more or less) faithful Chilkats. Their tribe had lived on the coast for years and jealously guarded the passes into the interior to keep a monopoly on the fur trade with the inland Indians. With a little persuasion from a U.S. Navy target practice with Gatling guns, they'd yielded a right of passage over Chilkoot to the miners. At any rate, Thunder and Lightning knew how to get over Chilkoot in any weather.

"Anyhow," Knucks concluded, "I'm out to spread the news, and I've done 'er, and to see that more supplies come up in the spring to take care of a lot more folks."

"I'll see to that," Cap assured him. Running supplies made as much for the *Idaho* as running passengers—and then some.

Later in bed, Maggie whispered in Dolf's ear. "I still say it was mean."

"What?" Dolf asked.

"What you did to Hubie."

He grunted. "In a pig's eye. I set the little guy up for the first fun he's probably had in twenty years. I wonder if Rupert stood for the treat."

She poked him in the ribs. "You are bad," she said.

He turned over and nestled her close, kissing her tenderly. Then he nibbled an ear lobe lightly. He whispered, "Hubie said there were bad men up North. I'm just tryin' to fit in."

"I'm sure you will," she said, then giggled.

CHAPTER 3

GOLDIE (or Rupert) Smith had acquired vastly greater managerial ability since he'd been run out of the Sky Pilot mining district in '87. The reason had been christened Nilda Carlson twenty-four years before. She was formerly a Minnesota milkmaid with the grip to prove it. Rupert hadn't been any more disposed to listen to her advice than to anyone else's until, in bed one night, she had applied that grip to his Adams apple and held him till he started to turn blue in the face. After she'd released him and he'd regained his senses, she tossed him a six-shooter. "Here," she'd said. "You may think you're gonna shoot me for that. I don't think you've got the guts. Go ahead," she'd goaded him.

He couldn't even look directly into her cold, blue eyes that were now glaring contemptuously at him—much less shoot her. He carefully laid the six-shooter on the dresser, blessing his stars that he was still alive and too stupid to discover she'd providently removed the live cartridges and replaced them with empties—just in case. It was that sort of grit and foresight that made Nilda a good manager. Another example had been the pearl-handled .32 "lemon squeezer" in her wrapper pocket during this encounter, with which she'd intended to kill him if he'd pointed the six-shooter at her.

"Now," Nilda had informed Goldie, "you'd better get the wax out of your ears and listen to me or I'll pop it out with a two-by-four."

The best Goldie could manage was a glassy-eyed stare and a vigorous nod of assent. His blood pounded in his ears, and he panted like a pooped-out puppy.

"Say something," she'd ordered.

"Yes, dear."

"That's better. We're partners from here on out. In case you thought I was letting a little lap dog like you get his jollies with me for nothing, now you know better."

Nilda wasn't big, but she was mighty, a substantial five-seven with an hourglass figure and legs like the Mighty Sandow. She had a deceptive, Lillian Russell baby face, light blue eyes with long lashes, naturally curly, golden hair, and milky white skin. Her smile, revealing lovely, even white teeth, had been the undoing of many men—including her stepfather, who'd had his amorous aspirations discouraged one day in their barn back in Minnesota by a singletree wielded in Nilda's capable grip. On the off chance that she'd hit him a trifle hard, she'd promptly thumbed a ride on a passing wagon and eventually spent the winter cooking at a lumber camp. Several lumberjacks also had learned what she could do—in this case with an axe handle—before they'd stopped trying the laying-on-of-hands to cure her of her virginity.

The next season had found her in Seattle where she got a job cooking in a boardinghouse and fell deeply in love with a cigar drummer. He'd finally dumped her in San Francisco where her peregrinations followed the "melancholy path of abandoned women"—as contemporary journalists loved to phrase it. She ended up in a Barbary Coast bordello, the pampered favorite of several wealthy clients. That's where Rupert had found her and, he thought, tolled her to the Land of the Midnight Sun with tales of gold nuggets as big as hens' eggs sprouting from the ground. He'd been unaware that his plans for her hadn't held a candle to hers for him—literally a case of "vice" versa.

Unlike Goldie's brother Hubie, Nilda had been enchanted with her first sight of the Skookum emporium. It was big and ornate.

"What does this joint gross a month?" was her first remark after Goldie had shown her around.

"What?" he'd asked.

She'd regarded him as if he were a retarded boy. "How much money do you take in during the average month?"

"How the hell would I know? Enough to pay the bills." He'd looked stunned and wondered, What the hell would anyone keep books on a joint for?

"We're gonna change that," she'd assured him. Thus, Hubie's arrival was a blessing in her eyes. Soon after the reception Dolf and Knucks had arranged for him, Goldie saw no reason not to take Hubie upstairs to meet her. Goldie and Nilda had their own apartment at the rear, furnished in a style that was a cross between late Victorian bordello and Siwash. The former was responsible for the backbreaking chairs and sofas covered with woven horsehair; the latter was principally useful for keeping a sitter awake due to itching from being pierced by broken and protruding horsehair ends. In addition, there was a sprinkling of fashionable marble-topped tables; wobbly, spool-legged tables; bookcases; a Brussels carpet, and a cut-glass kerosene lamp chandelier. Dust-collecting pictures were on the walls and there was an arch screened with Madras beads. The Siwash part consisted of a miniature totem pole, bear throw rugs, the figurehead and a paddle from a Chilkat canoe, parkas and mukluks as wall hangings, an "oosig" from a walrus, a jar of unpolished native black diamonds, a harpoon, and some bows and arrows.

A trifle pop-eyed over the confusing array, Hubie reviewed the crowded interior of the apartment. Then he laid eyes on Nilda and instantly fell in love. She gave him a warm handshake, carefully relaxing her vise-like grip into putty as she batted her big blue eyes at him.

"Hi, Hubie," she said softly. "I'm so glad you're here. I've always wanted a brother." She actually had seven of them.

Hubie only gulped; Cupid's arrow was firmly imbedded in his gizzard. He tried to keep his eyes off the generous cleavage framed by the feathery collar on Nilda's low-cut gown. It never occurred to him that she was a whore and dressed like one. He smiled lopsidedly, blushing.

Goldie was too vain to think for a moment that some sort of chemistry might be afoot. He looked around impatiently. To Nilda he said, "We can put him in the spare bedroom a few days, I reckon." To Hubie he said, "If you're hungry Nilda will fix you something."

He hadn't asked Nilda, but he knew he would get no argument from her on such small, domestic details.

"Are you hungry?" Nilda asked Hubie.

"Kinda, I guess. If it ain't no trouble."

Nilda smiled, and Hubie almost became unglued somewhere low down inside of himself. "No trouble at all. I love to cook. How about you, Goldie? I got a big moose stew on."

"Not yet, dear. I got some boys downstairs I want to see for awhile." He made it as casual as he could. He was gratified to note that she didn't lay a suspicious look on him.

"You go ahead, dearie," she told Goldie, and he trotted out.

"Have you ever had moose stew?" was the last thing he heard as he closed the door and, instead of heading downstairs, tiptoed rapidly up the hall toward the big front room. On both sides of the hall were girls' rooms, then a club room in front which he'd had furnished as an apartment to rent to some old associates. There was another stairway at the front end of the hall.

Back in the apartment Hubie was casting his eyes on Nilda whenever she wasn't looking, and was glad he was already seated at the oilcloth-covered kitchen table. Nilda filled the dress she was wearing so closely that everything that wiggled was visible—and a lot wiggled on Nilda, much of it on purpose. Hubie was too innocent to suspect that all she had on under the dress was Nilda.

"I hope you like my recipe, Hubie," she said, ladling him out a big bowl of stew.

"Oh, I'm sure I will." If she'd filled him with dishwater he wasn't apt to notice. She sliced some bread and placed it and butter on the table. "Coffee with or after?" she asked.

"After, I guess."

She poured herself a cup of coffee and sat down opposite him. "What do you do?" she asked.

He almost spit out a mouthful, he was so ready to oblige her with a prompt answer; then he nearly choked getting the mouthful down. "Well, I own a three-chair barbershop in Chicago, but I went to business school once and thought maybe I could get a bookkeeping job with my brother." He blushed. "Of course, I thought he was in a mercantile business."

Nilda almost guffawed. "I'm sure Goldie has just what you want—as a matter of fact, he mentioned something about getting a bookkeeper." To herself she said, "And if he didn't, he will. I'll see to that." She had her own plans for how a joint or anything else should be operated.

After he finished a second bowl of stew she said, "I've got cherry pie to go with the coffee. Want some?"

He finished two helpings of that, too.

Nilda thought, It isn't hard to see how he got so round. (Husky was definitely not the word for Hubie, as Margaret had concluded earlier.)

"I'll show you your bedroom," she offered.

He didn't see how he could get up even then, so he said quickly, "Could I have another cup of coffee?"

Nilda suspected the innocent little man's problem and deliberately brushed against him as she poured another cup of coffee. "Would you like to come into the parlor and drink it?" she asked, inwardly laughing.

Hubie blushed again. "Could I just stay here awhile?" he asked, looking like a speared salmon about to gasp its last.

"Why not?" She poured herself another coffee. "Tell me about when you and Goldie were boys."

Nilda had long ago learned that information was power. She would have been a lot less happy if she'd known where Goldie was just then—and what he was planning.

Goldie had just had the Skookum's clubroom furnished with beds, a couple of dressers, chairs, chamber pots, and the usual other amenities for comfortable living—especially whiskey and cigars. He was there now, sprawled in a big Morris chair, getting a fresh cigar going. The chair almost swallowed the dapper little con man. He greedily sucked at the cigar with fat, red lips formed like two sausages buried between his black mustache and trimmed spade-shaped beard. His dark brown eyes crossed a trifle as he touched a match to his cigar. He looked like an early Italian painting of a saint with his big, liquid, slightly-unfocused eyes.

"Well, boys," he said to his two old cronies. "It's like the old days at Leadville and Deadwood. I got a feeling in my bones we're gonna do even better here. One o' these days they're gonna hit a real bonanza up in the interior. They're takin' out a couple million a year now."

The other two were sprawled in chairs like Goldie's, each with a cigar and a glass of whiskey. They were striking contrasts: one a short, heavy, dark-haired and olive-skinned individual; the other a tall, lean blond with a guileless pink face.

Goldie raised his glass in a toast. "To the good old days."

All three tossed off their drinks. Goldie was getting on a pretty good glow. "The best chance for you two to get Morgette is probably right here in Juneau," he said. "But you'll have to do it pretty soon. He's likely planning to spend the winter up at his place in Dyea. You won't be able to get him in a crowd up there."

The dark man laughed. "I don't need a crowd. Just get me within thirty feet of him."

Goldie nodded. "I've seen you work. I know what you can

do. We may be able to set him up. Best at night even though it won't be noisy. Some sonofabitch may see you in the day-time."

The dark man was "Shiv" Filetti. He'd been a circus knife thrower when Goldie had first attracted him into his orbit ten years earlier at Leadville.

Shiv said confidently, "I'll get him." His beady dark eyes glittered from under heavy black brows. "I'll get him." The tone left small doubt that he would.

The blond put in, "If I don't get him first."

Goldie shifted his glance from one to the other, wonder-ing from the blond's tone whether there might be some budding conflict here that could upset his plans. But could read no resentment on either's face. They'd been partners before and always had delivered for him—as well as for oth-ers he knew. He relaxed again.

To the blond he said, "Either way, Schoolboy, it's fifty-fifty, and a cut of the big payroll up on the Yukon in the spring. And it'll be a lot easier to tap that with Morgette out of the way. And maybe even impossible if he ain't."

He hadn't told them the full story of his grudge against Old John Hedley and Dolf Morgette. It was too embarrass-ing for a vain fellow like him to admit. A couple years ear-lier when he'd tried to hijack the spring cleanup going out of St. John he'd been blown out of the water—literally. He and a crew of his cutthroats had commandeered the steamer *River Queen* to go after the *Ira Baker* which was carrying the winter's take out from the Sky Pilot diggings. Earlier, the owners of the *River Queen* had burned Old John Hedley's first steamer to the waterline even before she was completely built. Goldie, who had unsuspectingly walked into Old John's retaliatory sabotage the following spring, sunk when the *River Queen* mysteriously blew up in the Yukon off St. John. There had been few doubts who'd been behind the explo-sion, but no proof.

In any case, Goldie had damn near drowned and had been glad to get back to Juneau to lick his wounds. It had taken a couple of years to get up his nerve again, but the experience had not permanently blunted his avarice. Besides, the potential take was an irresistible plum. He rightly considered Dolf Morgette the most likely obstacle to a successful hit this time.

Goldie congratulated himself again as he looked over his two assassins. Schoolboy Mumma, forty years old but not looking a day over twenty-five, a consummate con man, dangerous as any man in the West. Better yet, he never killed with a gun and had no public record as a killer, hence wasn't watched by anyone. He killed by a skilled blow from behind with a slung shot in the dark.

Shiv Filetti was the same type. He was a product of the New York underworld who had come west for the bigger money of the mining camps. His circus job had been his cover. Though he'd knifed victims in crowded saloons he'd never once been so much as suspected.

Goldie thought, I could have brought in a bunch of gunmen—if I could find any game enough to take on Morgette—and even they might not have gotten the job done. He considered the alternate approach he'd chosen as a sure thing.

His last remark before he headed back to his apartment was, "Don't even tell me how you're plannin' to do it. *Just do it.*"

He was humming when he let himself into the apartment. Nilda was sitting up in bed reading a romantic novel. "Hi, sweetheart," he greeted her. He stooped and gave her a light peck on the cheek.

She frowned, pushing his face away. "You've been drinking again," she complained. "You promised me you wouldn't."

"Not much," he said. "I met a couple of old friends."

"You always do. You want something to eat?" Her over-developed maternal nature extended itself to him even when he wasn't exactly pleasing her.

"Naw," he said. "I'm dog tired. I think I'll just turn in."

He was asleep, snoring in a few minutes. She thought, Not much drinking, my foot! You're full as a tick. She sighed. "Well," she told herself, "living with him beats milking cows and pitching manure." She thought of his younger brother, Hubie, who'd finally got in shape for bed somehow. They were as different as night and day. She liked Hubie a whole lot better, but unfortunately he wasn't rich.

CHAPTER 4

HUBIE was having a restless time of it in his strange bed, and not necessarily due to homesickness. His fitful dreams, when he was finally asleep, all involved a typically unsatisfactory image of Nilda, who would somehow fade away at the most frustrating times. At other times he awoke and worried briefly over what mysterious evil fate might be in store for Morgette.

He finally decided to take an active hand in allaying his restlessness. Not that he was a strong believer in mind over matter, but after firmly deciding that he'd get to sleep or else, he finally slept.

There was a lot more to the little, fat man than one would have thought. Before he went to sleep he decided to contact the Morgettes and warn Dolf. Something suggested to him it would be best not to do so openly. He knew that Knucks Geohagen was a friend of Dolf's. Maybe he'd be around to the Skookum and could be tipped off.

It hadn't yet occurred to Hubie, however, that his brother was actually behind the plot to get Dolf. He simply figured a man in Goldie's position was bound to hear a lot of underworld gossip.

As with most frontier amusement palaces, business at the Skookum was dull till the afternoon. The bar roared into full swing at night. Consequently Goldie and Nilda usually slept till least noon. Hubie awoke early, slipped out of his room, and tiptoed around the quiet apartment. He could hear snoring from behind the closed door of his brother's bedroom, and couldn't help but wonder at the possible delights of sharing a bed with warm, ample Nilda. He thought, the lucky stiff!

That thought lingered in his mind as he dressed, then quietly let himself out into the hall, intent on finding someplace to eat. He figured there'd be a dining room at the hotel and maybe he'd run into Dolf or Margaret there so he could kill two birds with one stone. An idle notion impelled him to tiptoe down the hall. He heard nothing stirring, although he had an idea what could be found behind each of the several doors. Near the other end of the hall he passed a deep alcove full of brooms and mops that were dimly visible in the light from the wall lamp at the end of the passageway near Goldie's apartment. There was one more door after the alcove, then a back stairway beyond which was the clubroom door. He could hear someone coming up the steps, and on a sudden impulse dodged into the alcove. He waited for the person to pass him, but instead he knocked softly at the clubroom door.

Someone said, "Oh, it's you, Lobo. Where the hell ya been? We thought you might have decided Morgette was too much to tackle." A laugh followed from the speaker.

The newcomer joined in the laughter. "Sure," he said. His voice faded away, but before the door closed Hubie heard his added comment. "Hell, there ain't no risk when yuh shoot 'em right where the suspenders cross."

There was more laughter inside, then muffled voices.

Hubie's heart started to pound. He had a pretty good idea what that remark signified. He knew now that he had to get hold of Dolf—on the sly or not. Those men in that room were undoubtedly planning Dolf's death. It occurred to him that Goldie knew more about it than he'd let on.

Hubie thought, I wish I'd seen that guy's face. Then cold fear almost paralyzed him at the thought of what might have become of him if the man had suspected that Hubie had overheard. Hastening to get away, he awkwardly placed his foot in a mop bucket and fell with a clatter. He heard a door open and thought, I'm a goner. He was afraid to look. He concentrated instead on untangling himself, his breath coming hard.

"What're you doing?" a voice asked.

It was a woman's voice. He almost fainted from relief, then got up sheepishly.

"You're Hubie," the voice continued.

He recognized one of the girls he'd met the night before. "I reckon," was the best answer he could manage. She was dressed like Nilda had been the previous evening.

"It's cold out here," she said, pulling his sleeve. "C'mon into my room. I got my fire goin'." He thought of pulling away and running down the stairs, but just then the clubroom door opened and a broad-shouldered man filled the doorway.

"What the hell's goin' on?" he asked.

Hubie could dimly make out the face: broad cheekbones and slanting cats' eyes above a drooping blond mustache. The man had long yellow hair like the pictures Hubie had seen of plainsmen, and he even wore buckskins. Beyond him Hubie saw Shiv and Schoolboy in the lamplight.

Quickly the girl said, "I got an early customer. Sorry over the racket, boys. He tripped over a bucket somebody left in the hall."

Looking doubtful, the two killers crowded behind the big man, Lobo. Hubie's heart was in his throat again. He thought, I'm dead. They suspect something's fishy. He knew he'd never be able to lie to them convincingly.

The girl had no idea what was afoot, but, reading their faces, said, "He's okay. He's Goldie's brother, stayin' at the other end of the hall."

That satisfied them. "C'mon in," she said to Hubie and dragged him inside. He heard the three men laughing before they returned to their room.

She looked him over more closely once he was inside. "You ain't missed many meals, partner," she allowed.

Outside it was barely dawn, as winter was not far away. A lamp was lit. "I'll fix some coffee," she said.

"I was on my way to find a restaurant," he blurted. "Why don't I just go ahead?"

She suspected from the way he'd been eying her that he'd really rather stay. "I got a cold box with plenty of grub in it on the windowsill," she protested. "I can have some bacon and eggs fixed in a jiffy. Us girls all are allowed to cook in our rooms."

She put out her hand and shook his. "I guess we ain't properly met, have we? I'm Lizzie LaBelle." She giggled. "At least I am now." Back in Nebraska on the farm she'd been Beckie Brewster, but she wasn't about to admit it—at least not yet.

"Oh?" was all Hubie could manage.

She took charge completely. "Take off your coat," she suggested. "It's warm in here." She artfully brushed against him in the process of helping him get it off, then stood directly in front of him. She looked into his eyes, hers revealing what she was thinking. "I have a feeling we'll be great friends." She leaned against him.

"Oh, Lord," Hubie groaned, then grabbed her.

She thought, For a rube he ain't a bad kisser. Besides, since he'd taken a bath the night before, and changed his clothes and brushed his teeth this morning, he smelled a lot better than sourdoughs or sailors. She was surprised to find him a lot more solid than she'd expected, despite his well-padded exterior—especially when she'd got him out of more than his coat. She bolted the door. Returning, she concluded that some of his dimensions were very satisfactory indeed.

Hubie, whose experience with women was restricted to his wife, had never seen a pretty woman in the altogether, like Lizzie was when she returned from the door. His eyes devoured her. Then he got undressed and hopped into bed.

His face reminded Lizzie of the novice farm boys she'd

introduced to the Garden of Aphrodite in the first house where she'd worked. She slid in beside him and snuggled close.

"Not so fast," she said at his vigorous reaction. "Slow is better. I'll teach you."

Later, outside, Hubie tried to collect his wits. But even the cold air didn't help. Still in a pleasant fog, he pinched himself. "Did that really happen?" he asked himself. He was in love again and dazed by it all—Nilda one day, Lizzie the next. He decided he hadn't been unfaithful to Nilda exactly—and he didn't think about his haycock wife back in Chicago at all.

"Cripes," he said under his breath. "I hope I find Morgette before it's too late." He wasn't at all sure those three plotters in the room next to Lizzie's hadn't left while he was busy.

Realizing he was late, he'd turned down Lizzie's offer of bacon and eggs. "Maybe later," he'd declined. "Anytime," she'd said. There was something about Hubie that she had liked right off, though she'd been unable to put her finger on exactly what it was—besides being nice and innocent.

Hubie spotted the hotel's sign up the road and hotfooted it in that direction. He looked furtively behind him and was startled to see the three sinister men from the clubroom step out of the Skookum. He started to turn and pretend he hadn't seen them when Lobo called, "Smith, wait up."

Hubie stood rooted in his tracks, sure they'd somehow read his mind.

In the dawn light, as Lobo lumbered toward him like a grizzly, Hubie found him distinctly threatening. His eyes were almost yellow, divided by a hawk nose that had been broken at least once. His long hair was actually a reddish yellow with streaks of gray beginning to show. Hubie tried to conceal his fright, looking at Lobo's two companions to avoid the big man's eyes.

Shiv's appearance was, if anything, less reassuring than Lobo's. But Schoolboy was smiling. That raised Hubie's hopes.

Schoolboy said, "We figured you might need a hearty breakfast seein' where you just been." He laughed and was joined by his companions.

The last thing Hubie wanted just then was to be delayed, especially by these three. He surprised himself by saying, "I was gonna take a walk and have breakfast with Goldie later."

"Hell," Schoolboy said. "He won't be up till noon. You'll starve before then." He grabbed Hubie's arm in a friendly fashion. "We're headed up to the hotel for some grub. C'mon."

Hubie didn't see how he could refuse. Reluctantly, he let himself be dragged along. The first face he saw in the dining room was Dolf's. His back to the wall, he was seated with Margaret, Cap Magruder, and Knucks, his eyes resting steadily on Lobo. The latter stopped upon seeing Dolf. Neither spoke.

Knucks saw Lobo and broke the tense silence. "Well, look who's here. This is like a family reunion."

Lobo moved forward. "Yah," he said sourly. Without further talk he led the way to a table as far away from Dolf's as he could get. Dolf looked curiously at Hubie as he passed, but didn't speak, not sure what Hubie was doing with such a trio. His eyes warned Margaret to be quiet as well.

Lobo seated himself with his back to the Morgette table, a fact that would have told one less green than Hubie that he feared no harm from Dolf.

"That's him," Shiv said to Lobo. "The big guy with the fellow that spoke to you. By the way, what the hell was that all about?"

Lobo cut his eyes at Hubie and back to Shiv. "Later," he said. "I'm hungry enough to eat the tail off a skunk."

Hubie noticed Dolf lean toward Margaret and say something, once looking his way as he spoke. He wished he knew what it was. He was praying that his three companions wouldn't discover he was on speaking terms with Dolf.

Dolf's remark had included everyone at his table. It was based on an innate sixth sense that seldom gave him false warnings. He'd said, "Hubie's in bad company. If I read his look right, he doesn't want any of us to let on that we know him."

"Who are those other men?" Margaret asked.

"Old schoolmates," Knucks answered for himself and Dolf.

Dolf grinned. "I'll tell you later about the big guy. I've never seen the other two. How about you, Knucks?"

"Nope."

Cap said, "They came up on the *Idaho*. Both seasick all the way, or at least they kept to their bunks the whole trip."

Something about that set off an alarm in Margaret's mind. She said nothing, but merely took a good look at Shiv and Schoolboy. Some purely Indian thing in her recognized what it was in Schoolboy that whites invariably missed—a wholly deceptive appearance. She thought, I wouldn't trust that one any further than I could throw a horse. She decided he'd bear watching—for Dolf's sake, if nothing else.

CHAPTER 5

HUBIE and the three killers were still at breakfast when Dolf's party left the dining room. Hubie tried to keep his anguish off his face. A way to shake his unwelcome companions was simply out of the question on short notice. Then he had what for him was a stroke of genius.

"Where's the can?" he asked, looking at Schoolboy.

"Search me," Schoolboy said. He turned to Lobo, who'd been in Juneau for some time, and said, "Can you help the man?"

Lobo was happy at the chance to get Hubie away for awhile. He pointed toward the lobby. "Through there and out back."

At the door Hubie looked back once and saw the three in earnest conversation. Then he turned and spotted Margaret down the corridor entering her room. He almost loped down there and, looking hastily around, knocked softly on the door. Margaret answered it and was aware instantly from Hubie's look that something was wrong.

"For God's sake, let me in quick," he said.

She pulled him into the room. Dolf was lounging on a chair, all ears at Hubie's urgent tone. "Who's chasin' you?" he asked.

Hubie spilled it all at once. "Those three guys with me are plannin' to kill you, Mr. Morgette."

Dolf didn't change expression. "I'm not surprised," he said. "At least in the case of the big guy. I beat the hell out of him once. That's where he got that crooked nose. Just how do they aim to get the job done?"

"I dunno," Hubie said. He blurted out a recital of what little he'd heard at the Skookum. "Now I've gotta get outa here before they figure I'm gone too long."

"I'll check to see the coast is clear before you leave," Margaret said. She looked both ways in the hall. "All clear," she said. Hubie rushed out.

"Thanks, Hubie," Dolf called after him.

Dolf shook his head slowly, puffing his after-breakfast cigar. He looked at Maggie who was eying him with deep concern. She'd been looking forward to a long, relaxing vacation. "I don't know the other two," Dolf said. "I can understand Lobo Lafferty havin' it in for me. I shellacked him twice in the ring when we were in the pen. The second time was when I busted his nose. Maybe he hired the other two to help get rid of me."

Margaret made a shrewder guess. "Maybe someone else hired all three of them."

Dolf said, "Goldie?"

"Who else?"

"Maybe I'll have to pay a little social call on him," Dolf said.

"Don't you dare go down to the Skookum," Maggie blurted, then was sorry. She knew he'd go if anyone even hinted he was dodging a challenge. Since her foot was already in it, she charged ahead. "Let's just get on the *Alaskan* and go up to Dyea," she suggested hopefully. "Just this once how about side-stepping trouble?"

He shook his head. "This kind of trouble only follows a man if he side-steps it. We'd spend all winter wondering if some of those fellows were skulkin' around the brush with a rifle—maybe all three."

Margaret knew he was right. She felt the familiar, constricting fear for him in her chest and hated it. She was afraid she'd die if he got killed. At least she didn't see how she could go on without him—despite having a son to care for and a foster daughter in St. John. She offered one last desperation ploy. "Thunder and Lightning are back at Dyea. They can get their whole tribe to be on the lookout for anyone sneaking around."

She watched him and saw the familiar granite determination capture his features.

"It won't work, honey," he said. "I ain't gonna make any fool plays, but I'm bound to give them their chance—maybe force their hand. I'll have someone covering my back every second. I reckon Paul Brown is still sheriff, and I can count on Knucks. Cap, too."

"Do you suppose Hubie heard right?" Margaret asked. She realized it was a foolish question and quickly added, "I suppose he did. Lucky for us."

"Pretty hard to put any other face on someone sayin' they're gonna get me right where the suspenders cross. Especially someone who's got a grudge." He paused. 'Lobo'd do it, too. He was a buffalo hunter, then a wolfer. One of the best rifle shots around. But I don't aim to let him get a bead on me."

This only added to Margaret's fears. She'd have liked to dope Dolf's coffee and take him out of town in a steamer trunk.

"First off," Dolf interrupted her thoughts, "I need to talk to Knucks and Cap. Then I aim to stay under cover till tonight. We'll let 'em wonder where I am."

Good, she thought. What she had in mind was handier for her after dark. She'd been raised under a code vastly different than Dolf's. She thought the idea of "fair and square" was dumb. She'd been taught to strike first, swiftly and by surprise.

When Hubie was out of hearing, Shiv Filetti said to Lobo, "I hope you got a good look at Morgette. Who was the wise guy with him that spoke to you?"

"I know what Morgette looks like all right," Lobo assured

him. He had no particular reason to keep his and Dolf's former acquaintance to himself but saw no reason to reveal it,
either. This was typical of him. He ignored the question
about Knucks.

Shiv shrugged and said, "Goldie's brother's green as grass.
We'll have to be damn careful what we say around him. He's
dumb enough to spill anything we say to Goldie."

"That's a damn fact," Schoolboy allowed. "He wasn't so
dumb about finding a little nookie this morning, though.
That gal was a looker. I think I'll have to get a little piece of
that before long myself."

They all laughed. Filetti said, "In a whorehouse, look 'em
all over first. My papa told me that." He turned to Schoolboy. "Did your papa ever give you any advice?"

Coming from the stolid Shiv, the question startled Schoolboy.

Lobo said, "Maybe he didn't know his papa." They all
laughed again.

"I knew the bastard all right. The only good advice he ever
gave me was 'don't spoil a good five dollar drunk with a
nickel bowl of bean soup.' He sure followed his own advice—drunk every night and beatin' up Ma. I finally killed
him."

The other two looked at him skeptically.

"By gawd, I almost believe you," Shiv said.

Schoolboy looked as innocent as he usually did, perhaps a
trifle more so, and said, "You'd damn well better believe me.
It's a fact."

Neither of the others thought any less of him for it.
Motherhood was one of the few items of sacred belief to
which all three uniformly subscribed.

Filetti changed the subject. "And don't forget, Lobo, Goldie doesn't know a damn thing about us ringin' you in on
this deal. You just happened to drop in for old times' sake."

"Sure," Lobo said. "And for maybe ringin' him out." He

guffawed. "I oughta tell Morgette that Goldie tried to hire me to kill him an' let him put the little bastard out of the way for us."

"Good idea except for one thing," Schoolboy said. "We may need Goldie to bankroll us over to the Yukon in the spring. Depends on how the 'cyards' run this winter."

"I know," Lobo said. "I was only thinking' how rich that'd be. Maybe the miners'd get up a meeting and hang Morgette for us if he killed Goldie. It'd beat goin' up against him and sooner or later one of us'll have to."

"But not head on," Filetti observed. "Not head on. I'll lay you guys odds I get him tonight if he sticks his nose into the Skookum."

"No bet," Schoolboy said. "I've seen your work."

They were interrupted by Hubie returning. Filetti asked, "Did everything come out all right?"

Hubie thought about that a few seconds, then got it and guffawed. "Hey, I never heard that one before. That's a real leg-slapper. The boys back at the barber shop oughta hear that one."

Shiv slipped Schoolboy a look. The latter rolled his eyes toward the ceiling, but Hubie didn't notice. He was still anxious to get away from them. "Let me buy the treat," he offered. "Then I'm gonna take that walk I was headed for when I ran into you fellows."

The others were happy to stick him with the bill, and left ahead of him without so much as a "thank you." Hubie was so relieved he didn't notice. "I wonder if I should tell Rupert what they're up to?" he asked himself, then decided to ponder that awhile. As he left the hotel he thought, I didn't do too bad this morning—so far.

He hoped his luck would hold. It did. Although he decided on his walk to reveal the killer's plans to Goldie, his brother was out when he returned.

Nilda was in the apartment alone. He viewed her through new eyes after his experience with Lizzie. In the first place he'd learned that she was the madam for Goldie's upstairs enterprise. Or, as he'd said to himself when Lizzie had told him to keep his visit a secret or he'd have to pay up, "Jeez-uz. Nilda's a 'hoor' just like Lizzie."

Nilda could read the new confidence in him almost as soon as he came in. He didn't say, "Hello, Nilda," but "Hi, honey," and chucked her under the chin.

"You've been down in the bar," she accused. "Let me smell your breath."

He leaned over and blew at her.

"Hmm," she said. "No booze. What's got into you?"

He thought, Boy, if only you knew, I'd owe you two bucks!

"You've been up to something," she insisted. "Tell mama."

He wasn't about to tell her about Lizzie but thought he'd best tell her the rest in case she saw Goldie before he did. In fact, he was thinking of taking a long nap.

"Well," he started his story, "do you know anything about the fellers staying down at the other end of the hall?"

She shook her head. "Only that they're a couple of new gamblers Goldie brought in. He put 'em up there till they can find a cabin. Why?"

Hubie spilled the whole story except for his little excursion to Lizzie's room. He was so engrossed in his tale that he failed to note Nilda's expression harden, her eyes glinting wickedly at the realization that Goldie was about to engage in some huge—and stupidly risky—scheme without breathing a word of it to her. She wondered if he had her in mind for a one-way trip into the Lynn Canal some night.

When Hubie had finished, she said, "It's a good thing you told me instead of Goldie. Don't you know who put those men up to killing Morgette?"

Hubie looked blank. "Uh uh."

"Your brother, you dummy! You don't know him like I do. If you'd told him what you just told me he might have those men put *you* out of the way too. He's absolutely ruthless, believe me."

Hubie's mouth dropped open. In fact, he did believe her—except for the most important part of what she'd told him: that Goldie might have him killed.

She sensed his doubt and said, "Will you promise me something, cross your heart and hope to die?" She gave him her most appealing look.

He was captivated by her, ready for the woodpeckers to start on his head. "Cross my heart and hope to die," he repeated.

"Cross your heart and hope to die *what*?" Goldie interrupted.

Nilda never faltered a beat. "I was tellin' Hubie to stay away from the rooms down the hall. He's too nice. Besides, he's married." She slipped Hubie a wink and prayed he got her meaning.

"Christ!" Goldie snorted. "He's a grown man. Let him do what he pleases." Then added, "Only, not free. I'm hungry. How about you?" he asked Hubie.

"I'm sleepy," Hubie said. "Had breakfast, then hoofed it all over town."

"Go to sleep then," Goldie said. "Maybe tonight we can have a big confab about home."

As she fed Goldie his lunch, Nilda turned over the implications of Hubie's morning discovery, trying to figure how to turn it to her advantage. When Goldie left for a high stakes poker game down the street at the Nugget, she went down to Hubie's room. He was sound asleep. She shook him gently. When he opened his eyes she was standing naked beside the bed. He blinked.

She said, "I don't think any woman ever treated you right, Hubie. I'm going to be good to you as often as you like because I think you're nice. But you've got to listen to me and do what I say." By then she was beside him, stroking him gently. "Promise?" she asked him.

"I promise," he said hoarsely.

"First of all," she whispered in his ear, between small

dartings of her tongue into it, "I want to keep you alive. So you've got to promise you'll never tell Goldie what you heard this morning—or that you told me. Promise?"

"I promise," he panted. "I sure as hell do that." Then he grabbed her. After his session with Lizzie, he had a better idea of what he ought to do to her. Hubie was a fast learner.

When they were finally resting, Nilda said, "I found the wrong brother first."

Hubie couldn't think what to say, so he said nothing. He was wholly contented and soon dozed off. He didn't even stir when Nilda slipped away.

CHAPTER 6

WHAT Nilda wanted to know—had to know as she saw it—was crystal clear to her. She had to know why Goldie wanted Dolf Morgette killed badly enough to import three killers to do the job. (She was unaware Lobo was a volunteer.) Further, she was ardently curious to know why he was keeping the whole affair from her. She thought she knew the best way to find out.

She put on a new knee-length, red, off-the-shoulder dress that revealed a lot of cleavage, matching French-heeled shoes with bows, black net stockings, an innocent look—and absolutely nothing else except perfume. Then she went down the hall and rapped lightly on the clubroom door. Shiv Filetti opened it a crack and peeked out.

What he saw required one more eye at the very least, he thought, so he swung the door wide. "Well, well, well," he said. "Who are you?"

Nilda favored him with her most radiant smile and a great batting of her big blue eyes. "Goldie sent me to see how you boys are makin' out. I'm Nilda. Mrs. Goldie." She didn't consider either remark exactly a lie.

"Oh," Filetti said. "Uh—c'mon in. I'm here alone. The boys heard there was a high stakes game down at the Nugget and went down with Goldie."

Nilda thought, This couldn't be better. She maneuvered her way into the room with an exaggerated swaying of her ample hips and derrière, watching Shiv who was taking in her act with his piercing dark eyes. She was betting he hadn't had a woman in awhile. She swung around the room as though inspecting it. "I'll have the janitor in to clean up," she said.

"He shoulda' been here before now."

Shiv wanted a dodge to keep her around awhile, if only for her eye appeal—though he hoped for better than that. He had a good idea what she had been doing before she'd became Mrs. Goldie—if she was actually that. Goldie didn't strike him as the marrying type. For that matter, neither did Nilda.

"How about a drink?" he asked.

Nilda went over to the buffet on which the liquor and glasses—most of which were dirty—were perched in a jumbled mess. "Too early for me," she said. "Besides, I don't do it much. But let me pour you one. What's your poison?"

He took a bourbon straight. She poured him a big one. "Mind if I sit down?" she asked. "I been goin' all day so far."

"Sit," he said. "Stay awhile. I got nothin' to do just now." The truth was he'd have arranged nothing to do for about a week to accomplish what he had in mind.

She sat down and crossed her legs, showing a lot of Nilda in the process. Shiv's eyes bulged, not missing a thing. As a result he managed to pour some bourbon down his chin, wiping it off on the back of his hand. He didn't strike Nilda as a bargain, but she'd put up with a lot worse, and she figured he'd fall into her plan perfectly with a little manipulation. She uncrossed and recrossed her legs, seemingly unaware of his fascinated stare.

She said, "Goldie tells me you boys are all old friends."

"Yeah," Shiv said, his eyes gleaming. "Yeah." He licked his lips.

"Let me refill your glass," Nilda offered. She bent down to take it from his hand. She almost laughed at his face as he tried to see down the top of her dress. He was going to be easy. She handed him half a water glass of whiskey, then repeated the leg-crossing routine.

"There's something you should know," she told Shiv.

His eyes came away from her legs, and he looked directly at her. "What's that?"

She could have played up to him for a few days and found out what she wanted to know, but she didn't have time. She said, "Goldie ain't too bright. In fact, he doesn't have sense enough to come in out of the rain."

Shiv exploded in a short laugh. He said, "Tell me something new, sweetheart." He laughed again.

She joined him. "All right," she said. "Here's something new. I'm the brains of this outfit. We've cleared at least a couple of thousand a month since I've thrown in with Goldie—sometimes more."

That really got Shiv's attention. Money made a lot of sense to him. He'd figured out long before that the only times he'd ever been depressed were when he was broke or close to it. "You're gonna make a pitch," he guessed.

She nodded. Then she recrossed her legs. As usual, his eyes focused on that show.

"First off you've got to promise me you'll forget everything I say if you don't buy. Okay?"

He shrugged. "Will I have anything to lose if I do?" She was beginning to interest him as more than a pretty woman. He could almost hear her mental gears whirring. Unlike most men, he wasn't afraid of brainy women.

"O.K.," he easily agreed. "I'll keep mum."

Nilda knew that his promise wasn't worth much, but gambled heavily that he'd buy her deal.

She plopped herself on his lap. "I want to know exactly why Goldie brought you here. Then we'll take care of what's on your mind. After that we talk money." She wiggled comfortably, her lips close to his ear.

Soon she let them both into one of the empty bedrooms along the hall. If Shiv thought it was strange that the stove was going full blast in an obviously unused room, he didn't comment. Before long he'd spilled his whole story and a lot more.

Nilda had her man. She was satisfied that from then on she could call the tune with Shiv. Schoolboy and Lobo would have to wait. She checked the hall to be sure the coast was clear before letting him return to his room.

He was considerably richer and happier than he'd been an hour earlier, actually whistling under his breath. He decided to stroll down to the Nugget and see how things were going. Halfway there he was accosted by a Juneau institution that someone had named "the Hummingbird" for obvious reasons. He heard the humming before she grabbed him. He spun quickly, alarm on his face, afraid someone was trying to kill him. But he soon realized his mistake. She was a pretty fair-looking Indian girl, perhaps a little well-padded but far from homely. A few minutes before he wouldn't have turned down her proposition.

She said rapidly, "I no hurt. Hummybird want to ruv you. Fitty cent, only."

He laughed, fished "fitty" cents out of his pocket and gave it to her. "Maybe some other time," he said.

She smiled. "All same, maybe tomarra. You cute."

He went on his way whistling. He was thinking, Not likely, kid. Not with Nilda on the job. What old Goldie don't know won't hurt him—or me, either.

CHAPTER 7

AFTER Margaret let Hubie out of their room, Dolf resumed his relaxed position on the bed, arms laced behind his head. "I've been thinkin', honey," he said. "Maybe you could run up to Dyea on the *Alaskan* a day or two ahead of me to open up our cabin and put things in order."

Margaret carefully avoided looking at him, pretending to be busy locking the door. She was panicked and angry at his suggestion but concealed it well. If he insisted, she knew she would honor his wish. Or will I? she thought. Perhaps she could protect him better if he thought she was out of town. But where could she remain out of sight without raising anyone's suspicions? The *Idaho*, obviously, if she could persuade Cap Magruder to let her do it. She vowed to sneak off and see Cap privately as soon as she could.

"Fat chance of me leaving for Dyea alone," she said. "I'm keeping you right here in this room so someone doesn't puncture your lovable hide."

"Been tried," he said. "Us Morgettes don't puncture worth a durn."

"So you say. It seems to me you were punctured when I first met you—pretty close to dead, in fact."

"One in a hundred," he said. "I got a long ways to go before somebody gets lucky again."

"Suppose you get unlucky? I know why you want to stay here."

"Why?" he asked, seriously.

"You think someone'll say you're running out."

"You want me to run out?"

She thought that over awhile before answering. "Yes, yes, and yes—if you want to call it that."

He smiled up at her. "You called it that."

"No I didn't. I said you'd think someone would say that. Maybe they would. Let 'em."

She leaned down and kissed him gently, then fiercely. Then she drew back breathless. "If you died, I'd die, too," she said. "Did you ever think of that?"

"You wouldn't really. Who'd look after Henry and little Maggie?"

"Who'd look after me? I'd die inside at least. I think it's time you turned over a new leaf and started being an old married man."

He studied her quietly for a few seconds, sober-faced. "Lord knows I've been trying," he told her. Then after a long pause he added, "They won't let me."

She knew who "they" were. There were a lot of them: men like the three cold-eyed ones at that table in the dining room, others like Goldie. The reputations of Dolf and men like Dolf haunted them—probably always would until the frontier was tamed and the once wild towns got so that a cop in a blue suit could handle the trouble that cropped up. Even when men like Dolf weren't viewed as a threat, they were seen as a challenge: leaders of wolf packs doomed to be beaten and exiled, perhaps killed, by a younger and stronger contender. The thought frightened her. She couldn't imagine Dolf being beaten at anything, though she knew that it was almost certainly inevitable—unless she took a hand. She was planning to do that in this case, but she would need help. She would also have to deceive Dolf. She hated that part of it and wondered whether he would forgive her if he found out. She thought, I'll worry about that later and risk it so long as I can keep him from being hurt.

She nestled down beside him, putting her head on the arm he offered as a pillow. He drew her close and kissed her, pressing his mouth to hers for a long while. Finally he drew away and studied her face, tenderly looking into her eyes.

"You're really something," he said in a low voice.

"I hope so," she said. "What kind of a something in this case?"

"My maw, I guess. Or tryin' to be."

"Sometimes all men need one," she said. "Especially hard-headed ones—mentioning no names."

"I can take care of myself. Or at least with the help of a few friends in this case. I reckon I'll pull through. Why don't you run down Cap and Knucks and ask 'em to come here? I'll have one of them round up Paul Brown. As old Skookum Doc would say, 'I got a plee-an.' We'll give those monkeys a chance to cut loose their wolf."

She sighed, pretending to be resigned to whatever he had in mind. He grinned. She knew he thought she was coming around to his way of handling the present danger. Well, she told herself, I guess leetle Maggie is playing her cards just right—so far. Mentally she crossed her fingers—and a couple of toes for good measure. At least this would give her the opportunity to see Cap Magruder alone for a few minutes. Also Knucks. In the short season she'd known him up at St. John (actually, one fall through the next spring), Knucks had appointed himself as her surrogate father. She suspected that the meals she let him and Gabriel Dufan bum off her table may have had something to do with that.

Margaret had very little trouble talking Cap Magruder into harboring her on the *Idaho* after he learned what was afoot. He knew that her owls' eyes and catfootedness may have saved the lives of both Dolf and Old John Hedley right there in Juneau just a few years before. He asked her what she planned to do.

She shrugged. "Keep my eyes open, I guess. Yell 'look out!' if that's the thing to do. I can keep an eye on any of that rotten crowd on the street, especially at night when their kind are most apt to pull their dirty work."

"You got yore paw's coup stick with you again?" Cap asked, his eyes twinkling. He knew that a shot-loaded coup stick had been her chosen weapon before, when she'd knocked out a gunman slipping up on Dolf and Old John in the dark.

"You bet. And lots more."

"I ain't even gonna ask."

When she returned to the room Dolf asked, "You gonna be reasonable and run up to Dyea? The *Alaskan* pulls out in a couple of hours."

She tried her best to look stubborn. "Only if you really want me to."

He nodded. "I think it's best. Don't worry about me."

"What a dumb thing to say." Even knowing what she planned to do, she was angry at his remark. "I worry about you all the time. I even worry you'll catch cold if you don't put on your coat when you go out."

He grabbed her in a bear hug. Then he kissed her roughly, then lightly kissed her lips, the end of her nose, and both eyelids. "I really do love you a bunch, Maggie," he told her. "More all the time."

She had to blink back tears, pushing him away. "Let me go now," she said, "if I'm gonna get a suitcase packed. The others'll be here soon."

She was lugging her suitcase out of the door as Knucks and Cap entered. She winked at both in passing, since she'd also let Knucks in on her plan.

At the *Idaho*, she found the mate, Alphabet Tullywine (actually A.B.C. Tullywine), and told him that Cap wanted him up at their room at the hotel. She gave him a note from Cap. Alphabet read it, looked at her, and couldn't suppress a grin.

She'd had to fight the impulse to read it herself on the way down to the ship. "What did he say?" she asked.

Alphabet handed her the note. It read:

"Put the Dynamite Kid up in my cabin and do whatever she says. She's nobody's fool."

She told him to get her a sailor's outfit in her size, and an oilskin hat to conceal her hair. She also appropriated an oil-skin sou'wester which was a trifle too big, but which admirably concealed the fact that she was a woman. She deposited her suitcase in Cap's cabin after removing a couple of essential items and left the ship with Alphabet, parting from him a short distance uptown. She then loitered along the walk, carefully watching the people she passed to see if she got any suspicious looks. No one paid the least attention to her. Fine, she thought; I must look like what I'm supposed to be. But I hadn't better push my luck and walk past Dolf if he's on the street.

She wandered around the muddy streets, glad she was wearing a seaman's rubber boots. She wanted to get the lie of the town. Much of it was still covered with stumps from the trees that had gone to build the cabins dotting the site. The town was laid out on the coastal strip beneath steep, wooded mountains topped by sheer cliffs. Buildings were already creeping up the mountainside to the point where the incline became too steep to build. Across the Lynn Canal were similar mountains topped with early snow. She savored the tangy salt air, her mind momentarily distracted by the beauty of the spot.

She was shocked from her enjoyment of her surroundings by seeing Goldie departing the Skookum with two of the men she'd seen him with at breakfast—the large leonine one in buckskins and the boyish one. Nerves on edge, she angled across the street to avoid passing them too closely. It wouldn't do to have them recognize her. Her chest was painfully constricted; breath coming quickly and her heart pounding rapidly.

She pretended to look at a hardware display on the walk in front of a general store, but shot a careful glance up the street to see where her quarry was. Once they had a respectable lead, she began to follow them. They headed toward the waterfront, where even now the masts and cargo booms of the *Idaho* were visible over the low, intervening buildings.

Then they turned onto the dock and were out of her sight. Stifling an urge to run after them, she walked as quickly as she thought prudent. She was just in time to see them enter the Nugget Saloon, which was just across a muddy street from the *Idaho*.

What luck, she thought, I can keep an eye on them from on board unless they go out the back.

The suspicion kept entering and reentering her mind that if anything befell Dolf it would be at the Skookum. She remembered well the dank basement with its dim hallways and rabbit warren of rooms where she and Dolf had liberated their friend Jack Quillen from Goldie's hardcases back in '86. If Dolf ended up down there it would surely be to have his body buried deep beneath the dirt floor. She shivered, seeing him in her imagination toppled into a grave, his determined face stark-white and relaxed in death.

The frightening thought took her mind off business for a moment, and she almost ran into Lobo leaving the rear of the Nugget.

"Look where yer goin'," he snarled, but didn't stop. He was obviously headed for the water closet in a hurry.

She hurried up the alley and posted herself so that she could see Lobo return to the saloon without herself being seen. After he did she then went clear around the several buildings that adjoined the Nugget, crossed to the *Idaho*, and idled along the rail. Several hours passed with no further sight of them. Then she was gratified to see Shiv Filetti come around the corner and enter the Nugget, which helped reassure her that the others were still inside. She continued her vigil. Darkness was beginning to fall, and a misty fog crept in from the canal. The air smelled wet and was good to inhale.

She thought, I'm going to have to move closer or I won't be able to see them if they do come out. Accordingly, she went down the gangplank and crossed the street to the boardwalk that ran in front of the Nugget. She tried to see inside, but the windowpanes had been whitewashed and she couldn't see anything. She debated about going inside, but realized that it would arouse suspicion if she didn't order a drink—but if she did that, her voice would surely give her away. She settled for loitering by the wall of the next building.

Her eye was attracted to a woman approaching from the corner. She looked familiar, but Margaret couldn't place her at once. Then it came to her. That's impossible, she told herself; she's dead. But this woman was obviously not dead. Margaret watched as she accosted a man leaving the Nugget. He rudely brushed her aside. Margaret thought, she must be begging. She'd started to move closer for a better look at the woman's face when the woman moved toward her. A faint humming came from her as though she were singing softly to herself. When she was a few feet away, Margaret got a good look at her face. Then the hairs on the back of her neck stood up. It can't be, she told herself. Mama Borealis, mother of her foster daughter Maggie, had died in her arms over a year before. The woman looked directly at her, and Margaret involuntarily gasped the name, "Mama Borealis." Then she asked, "Is that really you?"

The woman stopped, then came closer and peered from beneath her hat. "Who you?" she asked.

"It's me. Maggie."

The woman shook her head, evidently perplexed by the sound of a woman's voice issuing from a person that appeared to be a man. But she wasn't afraid. She said, "How come you know like Mama Borealis? Dat was my sister up nort'. She all dead now up on Yukon. Gone up dere." She pointed skyward.

Margaret gasped. "You're Mama Borealis's sister?" She took the woman by the arm.

"All same like dat, sister," the other said.

"I've got to talk to you," Margaret told her. She switched into Chilkat which she'd picked up from Thunder and

Lightning. She told the Chilkat squaw the story of her sister, Mama Borealis, whom Margaret had nursed during her final illness, and whose infant daughter she'd taken as her own. The other hugged her when she had finished.

"You good," she said. "I love you." There were tears in her eyes.

Their talk was interrupted by the emergence from the Nugget of Goldie and his three sinister henchmen. Margaret heard Goldie tell them, "You two go down the street and me and Shiv'll go down the dock a ways and come in the back way. We can whipsaw the bastard."

Before Margaret could move away without arousing suspicion, Goldie and Shiv headed her way. She knew all too well who they'd referred to as the "bastard." Shiv looked hard at the Hummingbird but ignored Margaret. To the former, recalling their recent encounter, he said, "Hi, kid," then passed on. He said something to Goldie, and they both laughed.

Margaret told the Hummingbird, "I've got to follow those men. No time to tell you why. You follow the other two and let me know where they go. I'll meet you across from the Skookum." Then she quickly went after Goldie and Shiv, barely keeping them in sight in the gloom.

She heard Goldie say, "You go up first. I'll be along in a minute or so," and she saw Shiv split away out of sight. She decided to follow Goldie, thinking that he was the real root of her problem and the main threat to Dolf's life. She moved ahead, closing the distance between them.

CHAPTER 8

DOLF looked over his small army assembled in the hotel room, some of them of known quality, others not. Foremost was Paul Brown, sheriff by community consent rather than through formal governmental election. Paul had once tried to hire Dolf as his deputy. He remained a force in Juneau only so long as the community supported his actions, and Dolf knew that Paul sometimes had to tread more softly than he'd have liked. He was a seasoned frontier lawman who had begun as a Texas Ranger and then served several years as a sheriff in Colorado.

The others were Knucks Geohagen—true as steel, tough as they came, utterly fearless; Cap Magruder—of the same caliber; Alphabet Tullywine, Cap's mate; and finally, a seaman named Luna Montiero whom Cap recommended for his grit in any kind of scrape. As he'd said before Luna arrived, "He's seen so much trouble all over the world that a war would look like a vacation to him."

I sure could do worse, Dolf thought, as he looked over their determined faces. He believed in doing his own fighting, but in this case he needed tried and true friends to cover his back. They were now eying him expectantly, waiting to hear his plan. He didn't beat around the bush, nor did he think of asking for suggestions before he laid out his ideas.

For the sake of those who didn't know, he reviewed the threat and how he'd learned of it through Hubie Smith.

"I don't know for sure that Goldie is behind those three who seem to be out to get me, but it figures. I'd like to walk over and choke Goldie a little and make him talk, but from what Paul says, that won't do." He looked at the sheriff for confirmation.

"A fact," Brown said. "Goldie's been walkin' soft, makin' a big play for public support. Got half the saps in town eatin' outa his hand—lots of 'em on this payroll, most likely. I forgot to mention his front guy, Stanley King. King's an old timer, but a goody-goody. Doesn't cuss, doesn't drink, goes to church—he gives the gang a respectable appearance. He and Goldie are pretty odd bedfellows. There must be something goin' on there below the surface. Anyhow, a lot of respectable businessmen and honest folks listen to Stan where they wouldn't to Goldie. Together they're hard to buck. They've just about run what few miners' meetings we've had."

What he was referring to was the ultimate frontier authority in an area where there was little organized government. Miners' meetings had gotten their start in the California gold rush of '49, where their function was to try men apprehended by vigilantes. In the case of frontier Juneau, Paul Brown usually made the arrests for the miners' meetings, which considered only major offenses such as murder. Minor infractions and civil cases were heard by the Justice of the Peace, Blunderbuss Newgast. He'd picked up the name in California, where he'd maintained order in his court with a sawed-off scattergun.

Dolf said to Brown, "So old Stan King is in town? I sure don't need to lock horns with him just now."

"Where'd you know him?" Brown asked.

"Over in the Sky Pilot. I had to pound some wax out of his ears."

"What for, if I ain't bein' nosey?"

Dolf chuckled. "For makin' impolite remarks about my wife."

It wouldn't have been good manners for anyone to inquire further, but Dolf recalled all too well King's snide slurs about Maggie's Indian blood. In addition to being a pious fake, King was a bigot. Nonetheless, Dolf didn't intend to borrow trouble from that source.

"Well," he said, "we'll try to avoid anything that gets King and a miners' meeting down on me. Or at least in his case, down any more than he already is. But I'm not gonna let that cramp my style if it comes down to a ground hog case." He continued, "I figure these guys don't know I'm onto 'em. The most natural thing in the world'd be for me to stroll over to the Skookum with one of you after dinner. Almost everyone in town drops in there at least once a day, especially in the evenin'. That'd be their best bet to make a play—either in the crowd or when I went back. So why don't we pay a visit over there after dinner? I'd like two of you to cover the street with rifles while the rest of us walk down there. I may even sit in a card game—*with my back to the wall*. After we get down there, one of the boys with the rifles can mosey in. I'd like the other to watch the rear in case I have to go out back."

Cap put in, "Best we go there in a bunch. Remember what happened to Quillen? That's where they cold-cocked him and dragged him downstairs."

Alphabet Tullywine and Luna Montiero were chosen as the riflemen. They stationed themselves to guard Dolf against a shot from the dark while he ate dinner. Dolf and Knucks sat together, with Cap and the sheriff at another table to avoid suspicion in case they were being watched. For the same reason they took their time at supper, as though they didn't have a worry in the world.

Knucks, one of the outstanding boxers of his day, as well as a catch-as-catch-can wrestler, growled, "Why don't I go over and give Goldie my old whips-and-jingles hold? I guarantee you he'd talk like a Methodist circuit rider. We might even send him bye bye and feed him to the fish. And there won't be a mark on him."

Dolf shook his head. "Not just yet anyhow. We aren't sure that he's behind Lobo and those other two."

"Sheeit!" Knucks snorted. "Do birds fly? Of course he's behind 'em. We'll have to deal with him sooner or later anyhow."

Dolf eyed his friend amiably. "All in good time," he said. "I'm bettin' you're right, but let's not play that card yet." He knew only too well what Knucks referred to as his whips-and-jingles hold. He'd seen it applied to Little Pete, a Barbary Coast tong leader. Knucks had pressed his thumbs into the Chinaman's neck at a critical point, the little man's eyes had turned up into his head, and he'd flopped like a beheaded chicken. It had taken Little Pete half a minute to reorient his senses after being turned loose. And, as Knucks had said, he'd sung the tune they'd asked for like a true revivalist. It was something to fall back on as a last resort. But he preferred to let the actual killers tip their hand, then show them up and get them to point the finger at Goldie.

The four from the dining room went to the Skookum in two parties: Brown and Cap first to spy out the route, Dolf and Knucks coming later. Tullywine signaled a quick all clear from across the street when Dolf emerged from the hotel, but he wouldn't have had he known who the pair was that he'd seen go into the Skookum a short while before—Lobo Lafferty and Schoolboy Mumma. Cap Magruder, however, did know them, and, spotting them at the bar as soon as he entered, came back to warn Dolf.

"Fine," Dolf said. "If those two are in there maybe we can get the confirmation exercises started right off."

Cap preceded Dolf and Knucks back inside.

Despite a high ceiling, the interior was hung with a pall of tobacco smoke that reached just about to the height of Dolf's Stetson. Lamplight lent the room a mellow glow. Goldie had hung several kerosene chandeliers, plus reflector lamps along the walls and behind the bar. It was bright enough for

Dolf to survey the crowd from just inside the front door. Lobo and Schoolboy paid no attention as he entered, a sign of nonchalance that Dolf was unable to interpret. It certainly didn't signify a setup, but it could have been designed to throw him off guard. He didn't spot either Goldie or Shiv Filetti. Moreover, knowing Goldie's style, it wouldn't have surprised him if there were a few other hardcases positioned to ambush him. However, he assumed that there would be some overt move to provide an excuse to open the ball; perhaps Lobo would brace him to provoke a fight in which lead might start flying from any quarter—including the bartenders. They undoubtedly had scatterguns beneath the bar, a customary frontier precaution against the rough stuff that could start a free-for-all that was hard on glassware.

The absence of Goldie bothered Dolf, but then, Goldie was the type that was shy of danger. Dolf had expected to be greeted by the oily little con man; then, when Goldie moseyed off to the rear, Dolf had envisioned him giving the others the go-ahead if he thought the time was right.

Dolf was familiar with the layout of the Skookum. From where he stood, slightly to one side of the front door, the bar was to his right, fifty feet long and abutting the walls at both ends. The bartenders entered from a door at the rear that led to a storeroom—a handy hiding place from which to take aim at him.

At the left side of the barroom were several cloth-topped poker tables and a faro layout; a roulette wheel was in the back just outside the wide arch that led into the theater. The latter was about the same size as the bar; beyond it were a stage and dressing rooms. On the right sides of the theater, both in the front and back, were stairways leading to the girls' rooms, with the clubroom in front and Goldie's apartment in the rear. There was no second floor over the barroom, whose ceiling reached to the beamed roof, as did that of the theater. Down the center of both bar and theater were huge German heaters. The fog-dampened wool clothing of the patrons, (who almost invariably went immediately to the heaters) gave the interior a steamy smell which blended with the odor of tobacco smoke. To Dolf it was not unlike Idaho. He'd have associated this with happy memories if he hadn't been aware that violence was apt to erupt at any moment.

Satisfied for the moment, he moved to the front corner of the bar, Knucks following. Here no one could get behind him.

Lafferty looked his way, recognized him, then nodded slightly. Lobo said something to Schoolboy, not looking at Schoolboy as he did so. As Dolf expected, after a suitable interval Schoolboy glanced down the bar at him. Then he looked away.

"What'll it be?" Dolf asked Knucks as the bartender approached.

"Kentucky straight."

"Make it two," Dolf said. He aimed to nurse his usual after dinner "one" over a cigar. He gave Knucks a perfecto and lipped one for himself, slowly biting off the end, then lighting it to his satisfaction. Knucks did the same, tossed off his shot, then signaled the bartender for another. Dolf wasn't worried that Knucks might get unsteady. He'd seen him put away a quart in a few hours without staggering or slurring his speech.

"Place has got a smell to it," Knucks said. "Like a prize ring before the bell." His pale blue eyes darted around the room, glinting beneath brows scarred by many bareknuckle boxing matches. His red, Irish-whiskey face was set in a happy cast, anticipating trouble and relishing the idea. At fifty he was still in fighting trim due to ruthless exercise those days he wasn't on a bender. He tipped the scales at light heavyweight weight now, broad-shouldered but with an aging fighter's gut, some four inches of solid muscle. For years after he'd given up boxing he'd been one of the world's craftiest wrestlers. He wore his graying reddish hair in a crew cut that emphasized his sloping head. A large muscular neck bulged out from his shirt collar. As cellmates in the Idaho pen, Knucks had taught Dolf almost all he knew about boxing and wrestling. He'd said, "I'm keepin' just enough secrets to meself to set yuh on yer can if I ever have to."

He nursed his second whiskey in one large, bony-knuckled hand, and held his cigar in the other. He was not a gunfighter, but tonight he had a .45 shoved in his waistband. He could use it well enough if he had to.

Lobo and Schoolboy moved to the rear of the bar. Dolf kept an eye on them without seeming to. He actually expected the trouble to erupt from the dim interior of the variety theater where, since there was no performance, only a single wall lamp was lit. This was the only light in the hall that led outside to the water closets. That was the avenue by which Shiv, having left Goldie a few moments before, entered the barroom and, after glancing around, joined Lobo and Schoolboy.

"Here's your chance," Schoolboy greeted Shiv without preamble. "Morgette's at the other end of the bar. Stick him." He said it so only Shiv and Lobo could hear him.

Lobo watched Shiv's face in anticipation of his reaction to such an obvious challenge. Lobo would just as soon someone else take care of Dolf if it came down to it. He'd seen enough of him in the past. Of course, a rifle at long distance from ambush was another matter. The saying about him, back where he was well-known, was, "He don't miss."

Shiv looked around, noting Dolf's position to his satisfaction. "We'll have to wait till he moves," he said. "Does he look like he suspects something?"

"He always suspects something," Lobo said. "If he didn't he wouldn't have stayed alive this long."

"Well, when he does move, here's the way it'll go." Shiv slipped a switchblade from his pocket and rammed it abruptly into the front of the bar in one lightning move. It sunk deeply into the teak that Goldie had got at a bargain from a foundered ship's deck.

Schoolboy had seen Shiv make such a move before, but Lobo's face showed his surprise over the maneuver.

A moment later, however, it was obvious that something hadn't gone as it should. Shiv's broad, swarthy face assumed a look of annoyance.

"What's the matter?" Schoolboy asked. Then he could see that Shiv was tugging at his knife, trying to get it out of the wood.

"The sonofabitch is stuck," he grunted. Lobo had to struggle to keep from guffawing.

Shiv gave a frantic twist that was followed by a sharp snapping noise as the knife broke, leaving two inches of the blade still in the bar. "Uno, due, tre," he said. "quatro—"

"What the hell's that about?" Lobo asked Schoolboy.

"He's counting to ten in Italian."

"Oh."

At ten Shiv added, "Shit! I'm goin' upstairs and get me another knife."

He returned in a few minutes and ruefully regarded the protruding steel he'd left in the bar. "That was my best damn knife, too." He shook his head.

They each ordered another whiskey. Schoolboy sipped his, then asked, "Where the hell d'ya think Goldie's at?"

"Search me," Shiv said. "After we got down to the alley he told me to go ahead, he wanted us to come in one at a time. He was headed over toward the dock the last time I saw him."

"Well, he's sure takin' his time," Schoolboy complained. "Say—" An idea struck him. "He left big winner in the game. You don't suppose somebody followed him and rolled him, after you two split?"

Shiv laughed. "Roll that cagey little bastard? It'll be a cold day in hell if anybody ever does."

"What the hell do we do if he don't show up?" Lobo wondered.

"Get Morgette anyhow," Schoolboy said.

"I don't think that'd be smart," Shiv said.

"Why the hell not?" Schoolboy asked.

"You know Goldie. He calls the shots or gets hot under the collar. He's payin' for the show."

"Bullshit," Lobo snorted. "I don't give a damn whether I get paid or not. If I get the bastard in a set of sights I'm gonna plug 'im."

Shiv shrugged. "Suit yourself."

"I will," Lobo growled.

CHAPTER 9

MARGARET slept uneasily, one ear cocked for the sound of gunfire, even though she'd watched the Skookum surreptitiously from the roof of a shed across the street till she saw that Dolf had returned safely to the hotel. That had been fairly early, but she was satisfied, knowing he wasn't the restless type that might get up again once he turned in. She'd then waited on deck until Alphabet Tullywine returned for the night.

"All safe so far," he'd assured her.

So she'd gone to her bunk, more tired that she realized, falling into a deep sleep near morning. Now it was getting light, and she was hungry. She made her way to the galley where she expected to find Cap's cook, Hop Sing, on duty. They had become great friends during the Morgettes' travels on the *Idaho*. She heard him singing from far down the companionway.

> Buffaro gals wone-ee come
> ow-tone-eye, come ow-tone-eye
> Dance by ee right o ee moorn . . .

He was wonderfully off key, but happy. She smiled to herself, happy because he was happy. She could smell hot cakes and bacon cooking, coffee, and probably lots of other things as well, since some of the crew were staying on board. The rest, she knew, were probably upstairs at the Skookum or in the cabins of klootches who were cheaper than Goldie's girls.

As she entered the galley, Hop Sing looked up and gave her a broad, toothy smile. "Good morny, Mah-glet," he said.

"Wat you likee foh bleakfast? Ham? Eggee? Toast? Coffee?" He knew those comprised her favorite breakfast, but asked anyhow.

She suspected that he could speak English better than he let on but was simply obliging with an act everyone expected—and, moreover, slyly enjoyed his little joke. The fact that he always rhymed "eggee" and "coffee" suggested as much.

"Sure," she said. "You always know. I'm in a rut for breakfast." During her years on the reservation, and those earlier when her tribe was on the run from the army with little or nothing to eat, she'd become permanently starved. She ate like a man, yet never gained an ounce.

Hop Sing set her a place at his long worktable, pulled up a high stool for her, then poured her coffee. "Toot sweet," he said. She had no idea what he meant, nor that it was bastardized French.

While he worked on her meal, he intermittently popped out into the crew mess with food and returned with dirty dishes.

"Big whale out dere yestiddy," he said, motioning toward the middle of the Lynn Canal with his thumb.

"Oh, I wish I'd seen it," she said. She loved to watch the whales blow and sound. They always seemed intelligent and curious, watching her as she watched them.

"I see you wear sailor stuff yestiddy," he said. "Where Dolf?"

"Up at the hotel," she said. "Don't you dare tell him I'm still in town. If he comes down here, I'm gonna have to hide."

She trusted Hop Sing and told him what was going on, certain he would understand completely when he said, "Ah so, like tong bad guys Boo How Doy on Bobbly Coast."

She knew who the Boo How Doy were from what Dolf had told her about his adventure on the Barbary Coast. They were Chinese hatchet men—hired killers.

"Dolf come I hidee Mah-glet goodie," he assured her. "No worry. Back dere." He indicated his storeroom, then grinned. "Maybe in tayto sack—you plenty little."

She laughed, and he joined her.

He served her hot ham steak, four eggs sunny side up, and toast delicately browned with lots of fresh butter. Then he refilled her coffee cup and poured himself a cup of tea.

She was helping clean up after breakfast when a hubbub of excited voices swept in through the partially-opened transom. Hop Sing cocked his head, a puzzled expression on his moon face.

"'citement," he said. He headed for the companionway, Margaret following. Out on deck she drew back, remembering that Dolf might come, attracted by the noise. She saw and heard enough to know that someone had detected a floating body in the canal, given the alarm, and attracted a crowd. She decided to go to Cap's cabin, don her borrowed oilskins, and sally out to investigate. By the time she'd walked down the gangplank and edged into the crowd, the body had been pulled onto the dock.

"Holy cow!" someone yelled. "It's Goldie! Dead as a flounder!"

"Better send for Doc Meadows," someone else said. "If he's sober."

Meadows was coroner in the same way Paul Brown was sheriff—by more or less common consent.

"Get Paul Brown, too."

Margaret moved to the front of the crowd, confident in her disguise. She looked at Goldie's water-bloated face without emotion; she'd seen a lot of dead people, many of them dear friends and relatives. She had despised Goldie and now felt nothing but relief that he was dead.

Doc Meadows arrived and methodically started to peel Goldie out of his clothes. "Hey, ain't he gonna do that at the morgue?" a man close to Doc asked his neighbor.

Overhearing him, Doc said, "We ain't got a morgue.

Wouldn't stink it up if I did." He was obviously not one of Goldie's admirers. "Here," he said. "A couple of you hold him up while I shuck him outa his coat and shirt."

When the body was down to its underwear, a bloody spot showed under the ribs in back. Doc quickly slipped down the underwear with the help of two bystanders. The skin had turned a mottled pink, blue, and white around the edges of the jagged slit.

"Knifed," Doc pronounced. "A real expert job, or somebody was lucky. Aimed right under the short ribs. I'd bet it almost cut his heart in two."

"Here comes Stan King," someone said. Goldie's front man strode importantly through the crowd.

"What's goin' on here?" he demanded.

Doc said, "If you ain't blind it oughta be pretty damn obvious. Someone did Juneau a favor—I'd guess about dusk last night from the looks of him."

King glared at him with small black eyes under steel gray craggy brows. His face had a Lincolnesque look without the redeeming kindliness. He was aware of the resemblance and wore a beard without mustache to accentuate it.

"Matter of opinion," Stan snapped. "Most of us knew Goldie was good for the town." He looked around. There was a murmur of agreement. "I'm gonna get to the bottom of this murder and someone's gonna pay," he announced. "Who was with him last?"

Shiv Filetti, standing near the front of the crowd, was thinking fast. He knew that sooner or later the fact would come out that he was the last known person to see Goldie alive. He also realized that no one in town, and few anywhere, knew that he was an expert with a knife—so he felt it was safer to speak up than not.

"I left the Nugget with him and went up the street a ways." He pointed to Lobo and Schoolboy who were with him. "These two come out with us, ain't that right, boys?"

The crowd, sensing something interesting going on around the body, edged closer.

Shiv continued, "He left me right at the alley over there and headed this way. Said to go ahead, he'd be along in a minute. I figured he had to take a leak, so I headed back to the Skookum."

"What'd yuh do when he didn't show up?" King asked.

Filetti looked blank for a minute as though trying to recall. "Well, I went into the bar to wet my whistle. Lobo here and Schoolboy were already there, so we had a drink. I guess I mentioned that Goldie hadn't come in, but I figured he prob'ly went up and hit the hay. He'd been playin' high stakes poker since mornin' and left big winner."

At that King's face assumed a knowing look. "And who was big loser?"

"Search me," Shiv said. "I was only watchin' the last hour or so." He turned to Lobo and Schoolboy. "How about that—do you guys know?"

"We all lost some," Schoolboy chipped in. "There wasn't no big loser."

Stan King wasn't satisfied. "Did the game break up or did Goldie drag his haul and leave?"

"The game broke up," Schoolboy said. "So there wasn't any grousin'. He cleaned us fair and square."

"Where'd you two go after the game?" King asked, indicating both Lobo and Schoolboy.

"Back to the Skookum," Schoolboy said. "Only up the street."

King eyed him suspiciously. "How come you didn't go with this guy and Goldie?" He indicated Filetti, "Seein' as you were all goin' back to the Skookum anyhow?"

Schoolboy was thinking rapidly, since he knew that it would come out that all three of them were thick with Goldie. "There was a good reason for that," he said. "Goldie was afraid of a gunman in town that might be out to settle an old score. So he went the back way and asked us to scout the street and let him know if we saw the guy."

"Dolf Morgette," King put in positively. "Right?" But it wasn't really a question. King would have liked to figure a way to implicate Morgette in this murder, but knew no one would believe Dolf had either knifed someone or hired someone to do it for him.

"That's the man," Schoolboy said.

Everyone knew that Dolf was in town. His arrival anywhere was always big news—and would have been even if he'd visited New York City.

King's questioning took a new tack. To Filetti he said, "Did you see anyone around near where you last saw Goldie?"

At that point Margaret got the notion that it hadn't been wise to stick her nose into this affair, especially if Filetti recognized her. She started to move back into the crowd.

Filetti said, "I passed a little sailor talkin' to that gal, the Hummingbird. Right on the walk up the street from the Nugget, pretty close to the alley."

"What'd he look like?" Stan inquired.

"Well—." Filetti's gaze ran over the crowd. "He was short and wearin' oilskins." Just then he noticed Margaret edging away. She saw the recognition in his eyes a moment before he could say anything.

"That little feller there looks like him." He pointed at Margaret.

"How about it?" King said. "Were you there?"

Margaret's heart was in her mouth. Then she remembered Hop Sing's offer to hide her in a potato sack. She thanked the prompting of her guardian angel to put on a small pair of man's shoes, rather than the boots she'd worn yesterday. Hands reached for her as she darted away. One man grabbed her, but let go when she bit deeply into his hand. Two more barred the way, but she drew a long-bladed knife and slashed at them. They dodged aside.

"It's him!" King yelled. "He's a knife-wielder. Grab him!"

The surprise of her darting run got her in the clear. She debated heading for the buildings in town, but decided it was impossible to get there safely. On the other hand, to go on the *Idaho* invited trouble for everyone, but she didn't see a choice. She darted up the gangplank, almost running over Hop Sing.

"Go likee hellee," he said. "I slow 'em down."

She raced by him and ran into Tullywine in the companionway.

"Can't explain," she gasped. "Help Hop Sing."

On deck Tullywine took in the scene at a glance, grabbed a belaying pin, and joined the fray. Hop Sing had already toppled a couple of men into the water. Almost unable to breathe, they shouted for help in the icy Arctic sea.

"All hands on deck!" Tullywine roared in a bull voice. Then, beside Hop Sing he shouted, "Belay there. Stand back or someone gets killed."

A man in the front of the crowd pulled out a six-shooter and aimed it at Tullywine. "Drop the club, sailor boy," he ordered. Tullywine paused, measuring his chances, and wondering whether or not Margaret had had time to hide or change her garb. Then he heaved a sigh of relief as the marines landed behind him. He heard Luna Montiero yell, "Scatterguns lay over six-shooters. Put it away."

Tullywine glanced once over his shoulder and saw Luna with his double-barreled shotgun aimed out of the pilot house. Two men with belaying pins were coming to join the mate on the gangplank, and two Winchesters protruded from portholes on the deckhouse. Cap Magruder's ship often carried gold bullion, and he kept a crew trained to repel hijackers at an instant's notice. His prudence was paying off.

Stan King pushed through the crowd. He bawled, "Tullywine, yer interferin' with justice. We want that sailor. He killed Goldie last night."

Knowing who "that sailor" was, Tullywine had ample reason to doubt that.

"The hell you say? How do you know that?"

"Goldie was knifed. The sailor had a knife."

"So do I," Tullywine said. "So do half the guys in yer mob there. It don't signify."

"What the hell'd he run for then?" Stan wanted to know.

"Ask him. I'd o' run with that mob after me."

"Bring him out. And we want this chink, too. He busted two of my men over the head."

"Get up on deck," Tullywine ordered Hop Sing in a low voice. The cook faded behind him.

Stan King started up the gangplank. Tullywine halted him, raising his belaying pin. "Just hold on. We'll get the straight of this first. I never saw that sailor before. I don't think Hop Sing did either. But like me, Hop Sing probably thought a mob was after some swab and did what any white man would do. So don't go to blamin' him. We'll search the ship and find your man."

Stan King didn't look satisfied, but had no choice. Tullywine's offer seemed reasonable.

"Okay," King said. "Let's get with it. Some of you men come with me." When he turned to his mob several of the men surged forward.

"Hold it!" Tullywine ordered. "Not so fast. I want Paul Brown and Cap Magruder here first. Then we'll do this all legal and orderly."

King's face reddened. "Legal, hell," he snorted. "Brown doesn't pull as much weight in this burg as I do."

"That may be," Tullywine said, "but that scattergun back there pulls more weight around here than either one o' you just yet."

While this was transpiring, Lobo Lafferty edged out of the crowd and up the alley.

CHAPTER 10

NORMAN Ratsley, the hotel's mysteriously absent clerk, watched a figure in oilskins rush down the dim passage past the *Idaho's* brig. He was perplexed to see whoever it was quickly peel out of the rainwear, dump it out a porthole, then rush rapidly back. When he realized this was the author of his current confinement he was even more perplexed.

"What the devil has she been up to?" he asked himself. He wondered if her mysterious actions had something to do with the hullabaloo he'd heard outside. He hadn't been able to see any part of the action out his small porthole since he was on the seaward side of the ship.

Well, he thought, I guess I'll find out when the chink brings my chow. Or when I get out of here—if I ever do. Seeing Margaret, however, caused him to renew his pledge to somehow get even with her.

When the courier finally found Sheriff Paul Brown, he was in the hotel dining room eating breakfast with Cap, Knucks, and Dolf. They'd been in Cap's room earlier, which is why the messenger had missed Brown the first time he'd looked in at the hotel.

He hurried to their table and spilled out his news. "Paul, they just pulled Goldie's body out of the Canal."

Dolf thought, that'll solve my problem. He felt no remorse at Goldie's passing, being as certain as Knucks was that the little sneak was behind the plan of the three men to kill him. Now he could go and join Margaret at their cabin in Dyea.

Knucks spoke first. "I'll have to rush down to the church and light a candle for the late unlamented."

"Where's the body?" Brown asked.

"Down on the dock by the *Idaho*. Or at least it was when I left ten or fifteen minutes ago."

Brown got up, looking from one to the other. "You're all welcome to come along."

Dolf and Cap rose to join him. Dolf looked at Knucks. "Comin'?"

"In a minute. Damn if I'm gonna let the little stiff ruin my breakfast." He pitched back into his flapjacks between gulps of coffee.

Dolf shrugged and followed Brown, Cap and the messenger. Once in the street they could hear the excited mob on the dock. When they rounded the corner Dolf, seeing the mob being held off by Tullywine and the crew, was instantly on guard.

"Looks like somethin' else busted loose," Cap said.

"Here comes the sheriff," someone yelled. The crowd made way for him. Dolf hung back at first, looking over the situation. He could see what he assumed was Goldie's body, now covered by a blanket. Only the doctor, who was watching the action at the gangplank, was near it.

"What the hell's goin' on?" Brown asked Tullywine as soon as he was close enough. The mate explained in as few words as possible. Dolf caught the end of his remarks. "It wasn't any of our crew, as I told these galoots. Told 'em they were welcome to search the ship as soon as you and Cap got here."

Cap Magruder had something to say about that. "No damn mob's gonna traipse around my ship."

"The hell we aren't," Stan King burst out. "We're gonna get this murderer." He turned to the mob, filled with his and Goldie's toadies, and asked, "Ain't that right, boys?"

He didn't exactly get an overwhelming response. A good number of those who were eager enough with Goldie alive had started thinking about their futures. They knew who'd been making the payoffs and directing them to suckers—and it wasn't King. However, those who were simply interested in seeing a murderer ferreted out responded with a few words of encouragement.

Sheriff Brown held up his hands. He looked old and tired behind his gray walrus mustache. "Pipe down a minute, will ya?" he yelled. "We'll get to the bottom of this." The fact was, however, that he didn't particularly care whether they did or not. He'd been thinking of quitting a thankless job, to go back where it was warm and to raise a few cows—even chickens would do if he couldn't afford cows. But he wanted to protect Cap's interests the best way he could. If one of the men from the *Idaho* had killed Goldie, well, that was just too bad—and good riddance too as far as Brown saw it. If he'd rolled him, that would serve in place of the medal the killer deserved but would never get.

He said, "How about you, Stan, and about half a dozen good men that you pick comin' aboard? That okay with you, Cap?"

Magruder thought about that. Finally he said, "Suits me. I got nothin' to hide. Even if it was one of my boys, we'll turn him over to you, Sheriff."

Brown turned to Stan King. "That suit you, Stan?"

"Sure. Let's get with it." To the mob he said, "Some of you spread out along the dock and make sure no one makes a run for it. A couple of you get a skiff and see that no boat leaves from the other side."

While Stan was picking his men to accompany him on board, Cap said to Dolf, "How about you standin' guard here at the gangplank along with Luna?" By then Luna had come down from the bridge with his scattergun.

"Okay," Dolf said.

Cap, of course, had considered the possibility that if Dolf joined the search he might stumble across Margaret. He had no doubt who the little sailor in oilskins was.

"We want that Chink, too," King announced.

Cap eyed him coldly. "Like hell. You ain't gonna hang him for what I'd o' done myself just because he's a Chinaman. You get him over my dead body, is that clear? Let's settle this here and now."

King averted his eyes from Cap's cold glare.

"Well?" Cap said. "Spit it out. If you and your rabble here'd like a fight, you can get it right quick."

"Okay," King said. "Maybe the boys was a trifle hasty." Nonetheless, he was planning to make his move later if the opportunity arose. He considered anyone who wasn't white a personal threat to him.

Cap assigned a crew member to each member of the search party. He accompanied King himself.

Margaret could hear everything that transpired at the gangplank through the open porthole of Cap's stateroom. She thought of taking Hop Sing up on his offer of a potato sack to hide in, but she wasn't sure she'd find him in the galley. She glanced around Cap's room for a possible hiding place, dreading what Dolf would say or do if he found her still in Juneau. She looked at the Winchester hung on pegs over the door, but she didn't need a weapon to defend herself. Her best defense—the one that would embarrass no one—was simply to hide. Debating a run for the galley, she opened the door a slit, but was too late. Two men were coming down the companionway, checking out the cabins. Cautiously and quietly she closed the door and locked it. She heard them try it, saw the knob turn, then heard the sailor say, "This is Cap's cabin. I'd rather he was here to go in with us."

A voice said, "What the hell does he keep it locked for? Doesn't he trust you swabs?"

"How the hell would I know?" the sailor said. "I never tried to go in there before. We'll check it later."

She heard them move on and let out an anxious sigh. She

thought, I guess I'll just have to face the music when they come back with Cap. Better'n being found in a potato sack. That, indeed, would arouse suspicions. Perhaps Dolf wouldn't even find out that she was on board unless he overheard a casual conversation as the searchers left the ship. She had heard Cap ask him to guard the nearby gangplank and could see him there when she glanced out the porthole. She sat down, irritably glancing through one of Cap's books but not really reading it.

After some five minutes passed, she again crossed to the porthole and looked out. A movement across the way at the Nugget saloon caught her eye. Someone had quickly lifted his head above the false front and then ducked out of sight. It looked like Lobo Lafferty. Swiftly she crossed the room, stood on tiptoe, and grabbed Cap's Winchester. Her whole being prayed that it was loaded. She jacked the lever and saw that it was, then rushed back to the porthole. She aimed a the place where the head had appeared. No need to yell a warning to Dolf if she didn't have to, but if she did, she would yell and shoot both. This time the figure on the roof came up with a rifle and started to take aim. She was quicker, firing off a shot, then jacking in another shell. The rifleman, whom she was now sure had been Lobo, dropped from sight.

She yelled, "Duck, Dolf! There's a man across the street with a rifle!"

Dolf, who had turned toward the sound of her shot, spun around, his long-barreled Colt already in his hand. He was in time to see Lobo roll off the eaves of the Nugget and drop to the ground like a sack of meal. He could even hear the plop as the body smacked into the ground.

If the shooting had occurred a few minutes earlier, Stanley King might never have gotten to talk to Norman Ratsley through the barred door of the brig. Cap saw no way to shut

Ratsley up once he had King's ear, and stood by in helpless fury as Ratsley spilled what he'd seen Margaret doing a short while before.

King turned to Cap. "What the hell's your game here?"

Cap kept as cool as his hot temper allowed under the circumstances. He said, "It's nothin to hide, really. I hid the lady out because Dolf told her to go up to Dyea, and she didn't want to leave town knowin' some killers were on his trail. Can't say as I blamed her under the circumstances. That's why I put her up here and gave her an outfit to prowl around town in."

"What makes you think killers were on Morgette's trail?" King asked.

Cap couldn't see any way not to spill almost the whole story. He left Hubie's name out of it. To rub it in he added, "It figures your pal Goldie hired those killers."

"Is that what Morgette's squaw thought?" King's eyes gleamed wickedly.

"Anybody with good sense'd figure that," Cap said. "Especially with them three put up by Goldie at the Skookum."

King slapped his hands together. "It all fits!" he exclaimed. "She's an Injun. She was right there and had the chance. She knifed Goldie sure as God made green apples to protect her man. It's Injun style."

"Hold on," Cap said. "You're jumpin' to some damn flimsy conclusions."

"Like hell," Stan said coldly. "I want that squaw. I'm gonna call a miner's meetin' and we'll get to the bottom of this."

He spun on his heel to go back on deck. As he did, Cap felled him with the sap he always carried in his back pocket for reasoning with drunken sailors. He unlocked the door of the brig, pulled a six-shooter, and told Ratsley, "Drag him inside. And if you do or say anything but what I tell you from now on, you'll never walk off the *Idaho* alive."

They trussed up King and gagged him, shoving him far back under the bunk. Just then Margaret's rifle fire erupted overhead. "What the hell?" Cap said. He stepped into the companionway and locked the brig. "Mum's the word," he called back. "Or—" he passed his finger across his throat.

By the time Cap reached the deck, Dolf had started across the road. He was joined by Knucks, who had just reached the scene.

Cap hastened down the gangplank and joined them. King's appointed guards, plus others from the crowd that was still hanging around the dock, followed closely after Cap.

Doc and the men who had been carrying Goldie's body to the Skookum on a stretcher paused en route. They set the body down and stood gawking. Several voices chorused, "What happened? What was the shootin' all about?" Some of them had seen Lobo on the roof before he was shot. One said, "I seen the whole thing. That jasper tried to dry-gulch Morgette and Morgette got him—just like that. Must be a hundred yards and he picked him off with a six-shooter."

Of course that hadn't been what happened, but the fellow convinced himself he'd seen it. Soon, others who had seen nothing would adopt his story for the stature it would lend them.

"Good enough," Dolf said to himself, "let 'em think that."

He knew who'd shot Lafferty, and was recovering from the shock of discovering that Margaret was still in town. Under the circumstances, he was glad she was.

One of Cap's sailors joined the crowd, attracted from town by the racket. Cap grabbed him and said in a low voice, "Go tell Mr. Tullywine to get up steam. Then go round up the rest of the crew. But mum's the word to anybody else."

In the excitement, everyone had forgotten the search of the *Idaho*. Doc Meadows was checking out Lobo. "He ain't dead," he announced. "Shot bad, though. Mighta broke some bones rollin' off that roof, too. Toss Goldie's dead ass off that stretcher and help me get this one up to my office. I'm gonna to operate right quick."

It was more excitement than Juneau had had since the

anti-Chinese riots a few years before. Cap saw an opportunity to apply some mob psychology before anyone noticed that Stan King and his big mouth were absent. "Drinks are on me," he shouted. "Everybody up to the Skookum and we'll toast old Goldie—rest his soul." He almost choked on the words but knew how to influence a mob. He led the way. Behind him he heard excited discussion of the great shot Dolf had made. When he could get near Dolf, he said in a low voice, "You and Knucks better get your stuff outa the hotel and down to the *Idaho* the back way right quick. Can't explain just now, but I had to sap King to shut him up. He knows too damn much for anyone's good. Right now he's safe, but someone's sure to miss him pretty soon."

Dolf didn't ask questions. He gave Knucks the high sign and set him to work, then he headed back to the *Idaho*. Despite several fawning invitations, he declined to join the crowd.

Cap did the honors at the Skookum, buying round after round. When someone finally asked about King, he said, "The last I seen him he said he had enough of it and headed out to his cabin." He thought, that'll have to satisfy 'em. I sure as hell hope it does, anyhow.

It made sense to the crowd—typical frontiersmen who considered King's teetotaling a cause for suspicion. He had no close friends, though he was respected as an old timer in the territory. In any case, no one ever expected to see King in a saloon. So for the moment he was forgotten.

CHAPTER 11

THE crowd, by general consent, nominated Shiv Filetti—who someone had heard Goldie say was his best friend—to give the sad word to Nilda. The camp wasn't certain how solemnly the bond had been spliced in the case of Goldie and Nilda, but was giving them the benefit of the doubt. For her part, Nilda—a gal with foresight—had prepared for the possibility of such a melancholy event. She'd long before had a customer who was a forger make her a dandy marriage license. It looked more impressive than a legitimate one, and it stated that she was Mrs. Rupert Smith.

Yawning and stretching, still looking sleepy, she let Shiv in. She wore only a loose wrapper and, during her stretch, Shiv didn't miss a thing. The possibilities for him, with Nilda now unattached, had not escaped him. He'd been turning over how to play his cards as he walked up to the Skookum from the dock. He, too, wondered if the Smiths had really been married. If not, then Hubie would be the kingpin. Shiv laughed at the thought of such an innocent trying to run the joint.

"Hi," Nilda greeted him. "What brings you around so early?"

"News," he said.

"What kind?"

"Depends."

"On what?"

"On whether you'd be just as happy with Goldie dead."

Her face didn't change. Their exchange had gone as if it had been rehearsed, in case someone—Hubie for example—had been listening.

"He's really gone? How?"

Shiv explained. She said, "Sounds like a poor loser. Or a robbery."

Shiv said, "For all of his big mouth that guy King never checked that. I wonder if anyone else did. There was at least a grand in Goldie's wallet, and he had a poke of gold dust on him, too. I'd better go down and check for you."

Nilda was way ahead of him. "No hurry," she said. "If it's gone, it won't make any difference. If it ain't, no one'll steal it now. Doc Meadows is a drunk but not a thief. I want to talk to you."

Shiv sat down in the chair she offered him and watched her as she poured them coffee. She sat opposite him and put her elbows on the table, looking at him intently.

"How much did Goldie tell you about what he really had in mind for you guys after Morgette was out of the way?" she asked.

Filetti stroked his chin for a moment. "Well, I've got to admit, not much. He mentioned some big job he had in mind up north in the spring."

"Did he tell you where?"

"Nope. Only that it would be worth a lot and he was plannin' to cut us all in."

Nilda debated whether she could trust Filetti. He was a killer, she knew, but she'd known others and would have trusted the general run of them more than she would have trusted bankers, lawyers, or insurance men—even a lot of ministers. There was a down-to-earth, likable quality lurking behind Shiv's sinister exterior. She finally concluded that she had little choice. She needed a right-bower quickly, and wouldn't have trusted either Schoolboy or Lobo further than she could spit upwind in a cyclone. There was Hubie—good old Hubie—but she decided that he'd take too much educating and she simply lacked the time. Besides, she had other plans for him as Goldie's true heir—in case her phony marriage license was questioned.

"Here's the whole story. Goldie planned to hijack the spring cleanup on the Sky Pilot."

Filetti whistled, interrupting her. "Hell, that could be a million bucks. It won't be easy."

"Maybe not the way he planned it. He had some boys building a small, fast river steamer up at St. Michael. He was gonna do it strong-arm style, but he never was any too smart."

Filetti nodded agreement.

"And how're you plannin' to pull it off?" he asked, realizing she was waiting for the question.

"An inside job."

"A inside job?"

"Yeah. The cleanup'll be stored in the safe at Baker and Hedley's Commercial, just like always. They move the safe to the steamer in a wagon and carry it to St. Michael.

"How the hell do you plan to steal the safe?"

She laughed. "Maybe I won't have to. Just say you're with me all the way an' then I'll tell you."

"I'm your man."

"Goldie had a guy workin' for B. and H. He's an old friend of John Hedley's from Montana—more or less. Rudy Dwan. Everybody thought he drowned a couple of years back when the ice went out. But he didn't. I met him in San Francisco before I married Goldie—only Goldie didn't know that." She said the word "married" very smoothly and liked the way she managed it. "Anyhow, I found out plenty from a lot of boys that came in where I worked, and I filed it all away. This guy was no exception. With his help we may be able to pipe the stuff off before the safe is shipped."

What she didn't mention was that she planned to copper her bet by planting Hubie inside, too, where he could keep an eye on Dwan. To Filetti, she added, "We don't need to tell your two pals about this angle."

He thought that over briefly and winked, "Gotcha," he said, "What they don't know won't hurt us."

Nilda decided she was going to like working with Shiv.

She planned to move a version of the Skookum up to St. John on the first boat in any case. The town was getting to be known as the San Francisco of the north. She said, "Whatever happens, there's plenty of money to be made. I plan to keep our joint going and make a small mint whether the hijacking comes off or not. We might like it up there. If I do I plan to stay at least the first year and maybe stay till the bonanza runs out."

Filetti changed the subject. "If this guy Dwan is such a big friend of Old John Hedley's, how come he'd try to rob him?"

Nilda laughed. "Because anyone who knows Old John knows he'd do the same to Dwan if he could. From what I hear, Old John would probably laugh about it with Dwan over a drink once he got over his huff. Besides, they weren't always friends. Dwan worked for Goldie once before up there—a couple years back. Then he switched sides. It's a long story. Dwan's even in solid with Morgette. He saved Morgette's wife and kid from drowning, and everyone thought he'd drowned when he did it. Rudy just went back up there last summer. Morgette was in Idaho then, so he probably doesn't know Dwan's still alive."

"You sure as hell know a lot about everyone's business," Filetti said.

She laughed. "I listen real good. It pays." She added shyly, "That's how I know the end of your favorite knife is stuck in the bar downstairs." She watched for his reaction and wasn't disappointed by his look of surprise.

"Who the hell told you that?"

"A little bird."

He had to accept that. He laughed. Nonetheless, he wondered how she knew. He was sure she couldn't have talked to Schoolboy or Lobo before this—or was he? He wondered if she'd had one or the other—or both—in that spare room after he'd turned in early the night before. He wouldn't have put it past her.

"I'll never tell anyway," she added. "I wouldn't want to spoil your standing in the profesh."

Further conversation was cut off by the arrival of Hubie.

"Mornin'," he said, eying Filetti apprehensively.

"Hi," Nilda said.

"Hi, keed," Filetti said, and smiled, knowing that the little fat guy was afraid of him and wanting to put him at ease.

Nilda was wondering how to break the news about Goldie to Hubie. She'd observed his genuine affection for his brother.

"I've got some real bad news," she said finally, after fixing him a cup of coffee.

Hubie expected that the bad news would be from back home—perhaps the death of his wife—which, in view of recent events, wouldn't exactly have qualified as "bad news."

"Your brother was killed last night," she said.

"Rupert is dead?"

"Rupert is dead."

Hubie was too decent to notice that her eyes weren't even slightly red. However, tears came instantly to his own. He reached for his well-used handkerchief, blew his nose, and wiped his eyes.

"He was my favorite brother," he confessed.

That almost brought tears to Nilda's eyes. My God, she thought. What a family the rest must have been!

"Where's the body?" Hubie asked.

"I don't know," she said.

"What happened to him?"

Nilda turned the explanation over to Shiv. "Tell him," she said.

Downstairs, Goldie's body was being carried in and placed in the cold storage room with the bottled beer. Hank Trinity, Goldie's head bartender, ordered him put there and directed the laying out of the body across several cases of lager. He admired the result. "Sure looks right at home, don't he, boys?" he asked the stretcher men.

"Sure does," they agreed. "If he just had an ace up his sleeve and a cigar in his face he'd look natural as life," one allowed.

Trinity removed a cigar from his vest and shoved it between Goldie's stiff lips. They all laughed, then left him at peace, the cigar pointed skyward at a jaunty angle. Trinity thought, I wouldn't be surprised if he *does* have an ace up his sleeve. But he didn't go back to check. Like most, he wouldn't miss Goldie a bit. In fact, he liked him better the way he was.

CHAPTER 12

THE cry from the *Idaho's* brig barely drifted up to Cap Magruder's cabin. "Help! Let me out of here!"

Cap looked around at Dolf, Knucks, Tullywine, and Margaret. He chuckled. "As I was about to say, we still got a problem. That other galoot musta took King's gag off. I'll strangle him for that."

"Do you suppose anyone on the dock can hear him?" Margaret asked.

"Not likely," Cap said. "He's on the other side. Won't matter anyhow in a little while. I'm pullin' out."

Dolf said, "That's what worries me. Folks'll wonder about you pullin' out a couple of days early."

"Let 'em," Cap said. "I run my own show. Everybody knows that."

"What about when you head for Dyea instead o' the outside?"

Another faint cry drifted up from below deck.

Knucks said, "How about I go down 'n' give the bastard a treatment? I guarantee he won't squawk for a week."

Cap tossed him the key to the brig. "On me. Kick the other one's butt fer takin' that gag out 'less he was chokin' on it." Then, turning to Dolf's question about Dyea, he said, "I been turnin' that over in my mind. I don't think you oughta go to Dyea till the heat dies down a little. At least, not permanent. I got an old friend's got a place up the East Arm. He'll put yuh up. Lots o' room and he'll be glad to have some company over there to talk to."

Tullywine spoke for the first time. "Unless we pull over

there in the dark, someone's bound to see us. In a few days everyone in southeast Alaska'll know we were there."

"I thought o' that," Cap said. He looked at Dolf. "I reckon you got some stuff up at Dyea to pick up and take with you. You can get the Chilkats to run you over to Billy Moore's place with one o' them big cargo canoes. You said Thunder 'n Lightnin' are up there at Dyea. They know the place."

Margaret said, "We might be able to save some trouble all around and go up there in one of those big canoes right from here. Don't forget I've got connections after yesterday." She'd told them about the Hummingbird. "Let me go ashore for awhile."

Dolf nodded. "I'd rather not have people gettin' suspicious of Cap here. But be careful." To Cap he said, "We can take your two problems off your hands, too. Set 'em ashore with an outfit about halfway up, and they'll be two weeks walkin' back unless they hitch a canoe ride."

"You two may have something," Cap admitted. "Maggie, if you can get one o' them big canoes down here on the seaward side after dark, no one'll know where the hell you went. By the time King gets back, people'll be cooled down. Who the hell'll miss that little s.o.b. Goldie after they think it over? Besides, he was payin' the guys that yelled loudest in that crowd." He snorted. "I'll bet Mrs. Goldie fires that crew damn quick. She's got some brains. I wonder if she really *is* Mrs. Goldie." He noticed the perplexed looks he was getting from the Morgettes. "Oh—I reckon you two didn't know there was a Mrs. Goldie. He brought her in from San Francisco a little over a year ago. Big, buxom blond named Nilda. Nice gal. Lord knows how she got mixed up with him."

Margaret interrupted. "You men go ahead and talk about buxom blonds. I'm going to look for the Hummingbird."

Dolf yelled after her. "You got your coup stick?"

She popped back in smiling sweetly. "Yeah. And that ain't all." Then she left again, swiftly.

Tullywine looked at Dolf. "That's one helluva fine wife you got there. What'd she mean by that last remark?"

"Lord only knows—I don't." Actually, he did—and had mixed emotions about it. She probably had her .41 Colt and a Bowie knife. In fact, the neat incision in Goldie had aroused his suspicions, but he'd never voice them to anyone—least of all Maggie. He'd drawn the same conclusion Stan King had when he'd learned she hadn't left Juneau, only he wasn't as cocksure about it. Goldie had had a lot of enemies. He wondered if Goldie had been robbed and made a mental note to find out. If he had, that would point the finger away from Maggie.

After Margaret found the Hummingbird and told her their problem, she replied, "Prolly can do. I see. You come."

She led the way up the shingle along the Lynn Canal to the Indian camp—an agglomeration of packing cases, driftwood, and canvas shanties. Smoke from numerous cooking, heating, and fish-drying fires hung in the still air. Their approach was greeted by a committee of loose dogs that ran out barking, then wagged their tails and fawned for a pat or an ear-rubbing. In Maggie, they found their pigeon. She tried to pet each and every one of them.

"I take you to Big Cheese," the Hummingbird said, leading Maggie to the largest shack. She walked in without knocking. "Hey, Tunda," she announced. "Got comp'ny comin'." That word—undoubtedly the Hummingbird's best stab at "Thunder"—told Margaret who the big cheese was. He was seated inside eating crackers and cheese before a fire burning in a metal kerosene drum.

"Moe-gette Missus," he said. He jumped up and extended his hand, a broad smile capturing his moon face. "Where Moe-gette?"

Margaret wished she'd known ahead of time that Thunder, John Hedley's more-or-less faithful right-hand man, would be here. A certain amount of ceremony would have been useful. The occasion demanded a gift of his favorite frosted ginger snaps which he called "jingle snaps." She was fond of Thunder, even though he'd once tried to kill Dolf under the mistaken impression that he was an evil spirit. Once Dolf had straightened him out on that, Dolf had had no more faithful friend than Thunder. She was elated to see him.

It didn't take long for her to sketch the problem for Thunder. She ended her remarks with, "Do you think you can get us a big canoe by tonight?"

Thunder smiled, looking unintentionally evil behind his scraggly, drooping mustache. "You bet," he said.

Even if she'd never seen him before, Margaret would have bet that Thunder would have obliged her—as he'd be helping shanghai Stan King. All the indians knew that King held them in contempt. That was why Dolf hadn't been worried by the possibility that King would get back to Juneau and squeal too soon after being dumped forty miles up the craggy coast. Any Indian who might pass King in a canoe would be more inclined to drown him than offer him transportation.

Margaret had read the wicked gleam in Thunder's eyes at the mention of King, and his anticipatory glee over King's impending fate. He chortled, "Tunda take dat cultus fella bye bye heap planty. Take Dolf, Mah-glet to Dyea all same tonight—be dere tommarra."

"Great luck," Dolf said when Margaret carried the message back to the *Idaho*. "How is that rascal Thunder?"

"Same as always. A rascal," Margaret said. "We'll have to watch him so he doesn't throw King overboard in the dark."

"How about me?" Knucks asked. "Alright if I toss him overboard in the dark?"

Margaret shook her finger at him. "Not you, either. I'm gonna make an Injun-lover out of him someday." She grinned. They grinned back.

"Maybe we c'n git him hitched to the Hummingbird after you soften him up," Knucks suggested. "You said she ain't bad lookin'."

"She ain't for a fact," Cap put in. "A little well-fed maybe, but that can be fixed."

"Well," Margaret said, "he'll have his chance. We're taking the Hummingbird with us."

"Where to?" Dolf asked, suspecting he already knew.

"St. John," Maggie said. Then she reminded him, "She's little Maggie's aunt, don't forget. Besides, I can use some help with the kids if I start a school up there."

Dolf looked especially innocent as he grinned at her. "I don't reckon rescuing the gal from a life of sin had anything to do with it?"

"She needs a home."

And that, as Dolf knew, was that.

Their canoe, which was at least thirty-five feet long, was paddled by ten Chilkats. It easily held the Morgettes' effects, including the big hound Jim Too, King, the hotel clerk, and all the rest of them.

As they were about to shove off from the side of the *Idaho*, Tullywine yelled down. "I got one last thing you might need. Catch the end of it. I'll let it down."

In the semi-darkness, Knucks caught the end of a stout rope. Tullywine dropped the rest. "What the hell is this for?" Knucks yelled.

"To keelhaul that bastard King if he gets noisy again."

They shoved away in the luminous night, able to see the natives paddling swiftly and quietly in the starlight reflected from the snowy hills.

King was exceptionally quiet—as Knucks had promised he would be after a little treatment—despite the fact that he no longer had his gag in. Dolf forebore from asking what Knucks had done to him. He'd seen Knucks in the ring working on other experienced wrestlers and knew he'd learned some holds that brought pressure onto various nerves and caused either temporary paralysis—or the opposite. He'd seen the Irishman apply a knuckle to some part of the spine of a hulk half again as big as he was who was twisting his leg in an effort to maim him. The bigger man had gone flying into the air and had crashed down spread-eagled and helpless, whereupon Knucks had pinned him easily. Dolf also suspected that Knucks knew how to kill by similar, subtle means that would leave no trace—but he doubted he'd ever done it except as a last resort. Knucks gloried in mayhem but was not a killer by nature.

Next to Dolf in the darkness, Maggie suddenly asked, "Do you think we should go over to Cap's friend's place? I don't see why we won't be safe in Dyea."

Dolf guessed what her reasoning was. He knew she loved their snug little cabin in Dyea where their son Henry had been born almost four years before.

"Keep your voice down," he cautioned. "King may not be able to talk yet, but he may be able to hear."

"He's clear at the other end of the boat," she said.

"Anyhow," he said, "we'll talk about it after we dump our two passengers."

They had proceeded for at least five hours when Thunder indicated they'd reached the spot he'd chosen for marooning their unwelcome guests. After directing the paddlers to shore, he debarked and pulled the canoe up on the beach of an inlet. The Chilkats hustled King and the clerk ashore, left them a bundle of blankets and some food, then set off again.

"How long do you think it'll take them to get back to Juneau?" Dolf asked Thunder.

Thunder grinned in the darkness. "Mebbe so nebber," he said. "Mebbe so dat many day." He held up both hands, fingers spread.

Dolf wondered if the sly Chilkat had left his people in-

Join the Western Book Club
and GET 4 FREE* BOOKS NOW!
A $19.96 VALUE!

Yes! I want to subscribe to the Western Book Club.

Please send me my **4 FREE* BOOKS**. I have enclosed $2.00 for shipping/handling. Each month I'll receive the four newest Leisure Western selections to preview for 10 days. If I decide to keep them, I will pay the Special Members Only discounted price of just $3.36 each, a total of $13.44, plus $2.00 shipping/handling ($22.30 US in Canada). This is a **SAVINGS OF AT LEAST $6.00** off the bookstore price. There is no minimum number of books I must buy, and I may cancel the program at any time. In any case, the **4 FREE* BOOKS** are mine to keep.

*In Canada, add $5.00 shipping/handling per order for the first shipment. For all future shipments to Canada, the cost of membership is $22.30 US, which includes shipping and handling. (All payments must be made in US dollars.)

NAME: _____

ADDRESS: _____

CITY: _____ STATE: _____

COUNTRY: _____ ZIP: _____

TELEPHONE: _____

E-MAIL: _____

SIGNATURE: _____

If under 18, Parent or Guardian must sign. Terms, prices, and conditions subject to change. Subscription subject to acceptance. Dorchester Publishing reserves the right to reject any order or cancel any subscription.

structions to see that something permanent happened to King. He knew asking Thunder would net a lie.

Once underway again, Margaret poked Dolf in the ribs. "Okay, Big Chief," she teased him. "Mebbe so now you answer dis squaw question."

Dolf chuckled. "Mebbe so. Mebbe not. What question?"

"You know what. Why can't we stay in Dyea?"

"Because I don't want to risk a rope around your pretty little neck."

"Who'd come to get me?"

"The Navy. They serve warrants around here."

"That's not legal."

"Tell them. King's just the type to get a warrant out on you for killin' Goldie."

"But I didn't."

"Cuts no ice. I ain't gonna let you run that risk."

She was silent awhile. Then she said, "You think I killed Goldie?"

"I don't care who killed him—we can't take the chance of what someone else may believe. Goldie's friends saw you near where he was killed at about the right time and under derned suspicious circumstances."

That ended the discussion, Margaret knew. Even she had to admit the logic and sense of what he'd said.

"All right," she agreed. "We'll go over to old Whats'is's. But I've got some stuff I want to get at Dyea first."

"Well, I figure we'll be safe there for a few days, so there's no reason you can't do that."

CHAPTER 13

SNOW squalls forced the small coastal steamer *Yukon,* sister ship to the *Alaskan,* to move slowly southward along the east shore of the Lynn Canal so the captain could navigate by the hazy beacon of the dark, spruce-covered hills.

After a cold, wet, windy night of "siwashing" it in the brush, King and Ratsley were on a Stan and Norm basis. The prospect of perhaps having to cross a couple of glaciers and a dozen creeks and rivers to reach civilization welded a babes-in-the-woods alliance. Stan had spotted the *Yukon* first and yelled, "We're in luck, Norm. Start a fire and pile her on." His last caution to his companion was, "We can't let on how we got here. That ship belongs to Morgette's sidekick Hedley. Tell 'em we was up the creek prospecting and our skiff got away."

A few hours travel brought them back to Juneau, the day after they'd been shanghaied. If Dolf and Margaret had known this, their stay at Dyea would have been a lot briefer. If Cap Magruder had known it, he would have pulled out of Juneau for the States a great deal sooner.

Stan King trotted down the *Yukon's* gangplank practically dragging his companion and star witness. He was intent on finding Judge Blunderbuss Newgast. It was a fair bet he'd be at the Skookum's bar. King had viewed the *Idaho's* presence in port with great satisfaction. He continued to sport a knot on the back of his head, and it was still painful. The thought of Cap behind bars soothed his wrath—but did nothing for the throbbing reminder of why he wanted Cap jailed.

Blunderbuss was at Skookum's bar. King made a beeline

for him. He was only halfway there when he impatiently announced his presence with the words, "Judge, I've got some urgent work for you."

That caused every head in the place to turn. As Goldie had just been planted, this was quite a number. Frontier custom required a solemn, liquid tribute to the departed. The more-or-less widow had announced that drinks would be on the Skookum for an hour.

King looked around at the sea of expectant faces—not all of which he recognized. Perhaps someone would slip out and warn Cap if he blurted out his intentions. It might even be possible that Cap could have time to weigh anchor and steam up to Dyea to get the Morgettes clear of local justice; it would be just like him. King sidled up beside Blunderbuss and said in a low voice, "I can't spill it here."

The judge didn't like to be bothered at such an important affair. He tipped the ash from his cigar. He didn't know it, but it was the very one that had been removed from Goldie's dead lips by the thrifty bartender who'd put it there before the undertaker had removed the body.

"It'll have to keep—unless it's damn important," Blunderbuss said.

King was irritated. He started to say something angry, then knowing Blunderbuss, thought better of it. Instead he said, "It's important. When can I see you at your office?"

Blunderbuss regarded the remaining length of his cigar and figures out how long it would take him to smoke it. Then he estimated his inner thirst and said, "About three drinks."

This response didn't improve King's burning urge to revenge the indignities he'd suffered. Blunderbuss, he suspected, was trying to aggravate him. He restrained his temper with great difficulty, getting red in the face. Finally he managed to say, "How about a half hour, down by the court?"

Newgast scowled, removed a gold watch from his waistcoat, near-sightedly consulted it and growled, "How about an hour? Say 3 P.M." He also intended to have lunch first (since the funeral had caused him to postpone his usual noon meal), but he didn't mention that to King.

Margaret was happy to be safe and warm again in the snug cabin where she'd had hers and Dolf's first child. Memories swarmed into her consciousness. Nature had blotted out the terrible pain and fear of death associated with the Caesarean section which Doc Hennessey had been forced to perform. Only the happy recollection of the new being next to her after she'd regained consciousness remained. She remembered her first thought: he's part of me—mine—I'm a mother. She hadn't even wondered if it might be a girl.

Now, as she and Dolf crossed the threshold into their first real home, she was flooded with longing to see and hold their absent son. "I miss him," she said aloud.

She knew Dolf understood her. "I do, too, honey," he said. He took her into his arms. "We can hug each other for him, I reckon." They embraced for a long while, silent with thoughts and memories.

Dolf recalled the overwhelming panic that had seized him during Henry's birth when he realized he might lose Maggie. Then he'd known for sure that she was the only woman for him. She still was, and he was sure it never would be otherwise. He'd almost passed out from relief that night when Doc Hennessey miraculously showed up on their doorstep.

As a result of Doc's work, Maggie's midwife, Mama Borealis, had recognized Doc as Big Medicine and dubbed him Skookum Doc. But Doc hadn't been there the next year to save Mama Borealis from the deadly tuberculosis that took so many of the Indians in that inhospitable climate. Nor, in all probability, would he have been able to do so. Now Mama's sister was here with them. They'd almost forgotten her for the moment. She stood on the small porch behind them, happily watching their embrace, seeing how much they loved each other. When Margaret recalled that Hummingbird was there, she wriggled out of Dolf's arms and looked at her. Margaret giggled. "I'm sorry," she said to her. "I didn't mean to forget you. It's just that we're so happy to be home. Our boy was born here."

"Where boy?" the Hummingbird asked, fear dawning on her face. Her people lost so many children.

Maggie placed her hand on the other's arm. "It's all right," she assured her. "He's with my family. You'll meet him in the spring."

Then the Hummingbird smiled. She had her sister's faculty for love. As Mama Borealis had done, she also had decided to "adopt" the Morgettes. Margaret was impressed with how much she resembled Mama Borealis—including her arrival on their stoop with a pitiful bundle that contained all her wordly possessions. Margaret could hardly wait to make her a full-fledged member of the Morgette Family.

Watching Maggie's face, Dolf divined her thoughts and recognized that he shared them. He wondered if he'd only learned to be that way since he'd met Maggie, but couldn't decide. In any case, he was pleased. The grin brought to his face by the sight of those two proved it.

"I'll go in and get the stoves goin'," he said.

The two women followed. Shortly Maggie was showing her new sister the two big kitchen cupboards with their built-in flour sifters and many shelves and drawers.

"Any coffee still in there?" Dolf asked.

"Lots of canned stuff," Maggie said. "I can probably scratch up a meal."

She was only moderately surprised that their larder hadn't been cleaned out by the starving Chilkats. While it was true that Old John's trading post next door had been continuously operated by his brother Rafe, it would have been impossible to guard constantly against pilfering. Margaret knew there was another reason for the sanctity of their premises:

the superstitious tribesmen regarded Dolf as Big Medicine, and, moreover, associated Skookum Doc with Dolf. (Doc, they knew, was a shaman. He'd done such things as painlessly remove Hoonah Charlie's abscessed tooth and make the native medicine man laugh in the bargain. At will he could, remove all his own teeth and hair.) Thus, Maggie could prepare a meal with a main course of canned ham and baked beans, and had only to get the makings of fresh bread from the trading post. But there weren't to be as many meals there as she had hoped.

That night in bed, with Dolf's big hound, Jim Too, back at his favorite guard post beside them on the floor, Margaret expressed her optimistic feelings to Dolf. "Old King won't do anything, even when he gets back to town. Or, if he does, no one will pay any attention to him. I'll bet on it."

Dolf remained quiet, turning what she said over in his mind. He suspected what she was leading up to.

"Why don't we just stay here like we planned to?"

He was always inclined to please her if he could. Why not? he asked himself. His main reservation was based on his belief in King's vindictiveness. He knew that, as in the past, if Blunderbuss Newgast issued warrants for him and Maggie, the Navy would serve them if it could, without niggling over the finer points of legality. The Navy was, in fact, a law unto itself in this remote spot; resistance would be useless. The only escape would be flight. And in this season, flight was almost certainly out of the question. The Chilkoot Pass, their only potential escape route, was scarcely passable after the first snow. As far as Dolf knew, Knucks, Thunder, and Lightning were the only ones ever to make it across from the Yukon side—in this season. On the crest the winds frequently blew in excess of one hundred miles an hour; the snow was sharp as sand, blinding one so that at times a hand couldn't be seen before one's face. The cold could freeze exposed skin in less than a minute.

Considering this, Dolf replied finally, "I don't think we'd better risk it. We've probably got three or four safe days at the most. Then we'd better do as Cap suggested and mosey on over to Moore's place. I'm not sure we shouldn't have gone back outside on the *Idaho* with Cap. We could see our son. You miss him already. So do I."

Maggie considered his last statement first. "Father might not understand if we come back after leaving him. He'd think we don't trust him. I know him."

"Well," Dolf said, "we could spend the winter in San Francisco. Will Alexander would like that." He didn't mention Will's warm-hearted wife Clemmy, who would have liked it even better.

"I want to stay up here, now that we're here," Margaret said. "four days is better than nothing. I feel like we're home."

Luckily, she was unaware that they weren't to have four days, or even three. She went to sleep, utterly content and feeling safe, as she always did, on Dolf's shoulder. Later, as she turned on her side, half awake, Dolf automatically turned to nestle against her, one large arm encircling her, all without waking himself. She sighed and was soon sound asleep again.

Several curious men followed Stan King down to Blunderbuss's court. King looked back at them resentfully once or twice, but knew there was no way to prevent them from following him. He was sorry he'd blurted out the words that had alerted them. Most suspected that what he was about to reveal had something to do with Goldie's mysterious murder.

Blunderbuss was his own bailiff most of the time. He dispensed with the usual "hear ye's" and "this honorable court" and got right down to the nub of things. Ensconced behind his desk, he eyed King and the curious crowd amiably.

"Okay, Stan," he opened up. "Now what the hell's bitin' you?"

King would rather not have said, but it was now or never. He pointed to Norm Ratsley. "Me an' him know who killed Goldie. Not only that, but both of us were kidnapped."

Blunderbuss thought that over and concluded that it would have been a blessing if whoever had done it had seen that both of them stayed kidnapped. As for Goldie's murder, he considered it a blessing for which someone was due the thanks of the community—possibly even a medal. He concluded he was about to learn who the secret benefactor had been—or at least King's idea about the affair.

"All right," Blunderbuss said. "Consider yourself sworn and we'll take yer affidavit in this here matter. Who do you claim beefed the little skunk?"

King's expression registered his resentment at the way in which Blunderbuss stated the case. Though he'd been tempted to say the same thing when he'd administered the solemn last rites at Goldie's grave a few hours before. Instead, he'd put it ambiguously, referring tongue-in-cheek to "How we all know of the departed's many Christian virtues," and "how we now consign the late lamented" (he'd had an almost overpowering urge to substitute "the little son-of-a-bitch" for "late lamented") "back to the mysterious power that granted him life and controls the destinies of us all."

Nilda, Goldie's more-or-less widow, had dabbed politely at her eyes, thinking that at last she was now rich—or close to it. She was glad to accept the "late"; the "lamented" she left to his nice, fat brother Hubie, the true heir, who seemed genuinely grieved.

Back in court King was saying, "That Injun gal of Morgette's done Goldie in. Norm, you tell the judge who that fella in the yellow slicker was who was after Goldie just before he was knifed."

The clerk dutifully told how, from his observation post in

the *Idaho's* brig, he'd seen Margaret hastily shuck an identical outfit the very morning she'd fled on board from the mob.

In due course Shiv Filetti was found, and he testified under oath that he'd seen a similarly garbed figure the night before near where Goldie had been killed.

Blunderbuss brought up a point that didn't please King. "Why would she do a dumb thing like that?" he asked. "What was her motive?"

King was pulled up short. Finally he blurted, "Injuns don't need motives. She probably figured Goldie was her husband's enemy. Maybe she robbed him. Somebody did. He was cleaned when we found him."

"How come you know that?" Blunderbuss asked.

King looked uncomfortable. He wondered if anyone had noticed that he hadn't actually checked that right off, and decided to risk lying. "I looked for his poke first thing," he said, noticing Shiv's eyes on him as he did. Relief flooded him when he saw Shiv grin.

"We'll have to think that murder business over," Blunderbuss concluded. "Morgette's wife sure don't need money, so robbery won't do for a motive, and no one saw her actually do the job."

King blurted, "What the hell was she doin' runnin' around in a man's outfit? Why did she run when she was recognized the next morning? She's guilty as hell about something."

"Shut up!" Blunderbuss snapped. "Yer outa order. 'About something' don't necessarily mean about killin' Goldie. Like I said, we'll think that over. Now, let's get on to this kidnapping allegation."

There were a good many surprised murmurs in the crowd when King and Ratsley recited their tale of woe about being abducted. Also, a couple of snorts when King described how he'd been sapped. The J.P. asked, "How do you know who sapped you if he was behind you?"

King snapped, "He was the only one there. Besides, my pard here saw him do it, ain't that right?" He pointed to Norm, who nodded affirmation.

Someone in the crowd guffawed again. To a man they'd have liked to have been there to see Cap coldcock King.

"Order in this here court," Blunderbuss said, not very convincingly. "Now we're gonna adjourn for awhile and take these charges under advisement. Clear the court."

Actually, Blunderbuss was stalling for time to get a message down to Cap Magruder that he'd better get the hell out to sea. King suspected as much.

"Ain't you gonna have Cap pulled in before he skins out?" King snapped.

"All in due time," Blunderbuss said. "You can't jump on a ship and skedaddle like it was a hoss. He'll be there when I want him." As a matter of fact, he'd seen Luna Montiero, who'd been in the back among the spectators, slip out the door. "I want you two here while I write out yer affidavits to get 'em signed right off," he ordered King and Norm. "So don't be runnin' away."

He labored over pencil drafts, chewing his pencil and rumpling his shock of white hair, all the while humming to himself. Then he read his work to the two witnesses and, writing slowly and carefully in ink meticulously transferred the drafts to the official forms. All the while he knew that King was fidgeting furiously in his chair. When he finished he leisurely lit a cigar and looked over at the two witnesses.

"Okay, boys," he said. "Read 'em over again and if they're correct, sign 'em."

While King scanned his affidavit hastily, Blunderbuss heard what he'd been waiting for. The *Idaho's* whistle blasted its deep, mellow sound across the water, its echo reverberating from the hills. Soon the ship would be in deep water, getting up headway.

"Goddammit!" King almost shouted. "You let 'em get away."

Even Blunderbuss was shocked—but only at the source, not at the words, which he had to agree stated his intention admirably. However, he presented an aggrieved face to King.

"Why the hell didn't you two come in yesterday?" he asked.

King sputtered," You know why we didn't come in yesterday. It's in these papers. We was abducted."

Ratsley looked both puzzled and shocked: He had the notion that abduction was a weird perversion. "Don't get me involved in something like that!" he blurted.

King and Blunderbuss looked at him, startled. "Waddya mean?" King cried. "You was up to your ears in it! It's all in these affidavits."

"Then I ain't signin' nuthin! I wasn't abducted."

King was about to explode. Then he figured out the problem. " 'Abducted' means the same as 'kidnapped,' " he said patiently. "What'd you think it meant?"

"I dunno," Ratsley hedged, embarrassed. "But I was kidnapped all right." He signed his affidavit quickly.

Half a mile away, the *Idaho* was approaching cruising speed, a plume of heavy black smoke issuing from her stack.

CHAPTER 14

DOLF was proven wrong about the impossibility of getting over Chilkoot Pass at that season. The proof, however, involved what was close to a miracle.

Thunder and Lightning, hunting up along the frozen Dyea River, spotted figures moving high above them on the snowy slopes. These didn't appear to be game animals; no animals were apt to be that high then. They concluded these had to be humans, though they were sure no one from the village would be crazy enough to be up there. Then a snow squall blotted them out. But by then they were sure that what they'd seen had been two humans with dogs and a sled. Sleds were still not common, having been introduced only a few years ago by the Canucks Old John Hedley had brought over from Canada. Since then, however, both Indians had seen Old John's dog teams up on the Yukon and in Dyea, and had learned to handle one themselves.

"Somebody prob'ly needs help," Thunder said.

Lightning agreed, adding, "Plenty big damn fool to be up there."

Since no one could have gone up from their side without their hearing about it, they were faced with the incredible fact that whoever it was had come form the interior.

They slogged rapidly up the trail on snowshoes, knowing they couldn't miss their target. There was only one feasible trail. Actually, in spots there was no trail at all—just a crossing and re-crossing of the frozen river. They finally converged on the travelers and their gaunt dogs who were stumbling stubbornly along, obviously fagged out. The larger man was breaking trail, the other on the gee pole at the sled's rear. Just as they came in sight, they fell off the trail and tumbled through snow-covered brush onto the river ice.

A blue streak of oaths in a mixture of French, English, and Chinook burst out from beneath the parka hood of the leader. Thunder poked Lightning in the ribs. "I bet we know that one," he observed in his own tongue. It would have been surprising if he hadn't, considering how few men lived in the interior. But the sulfurous torrent of profanity marked this one from all the others.

Lightning agreed. "Yah. Mo-gette's friend Gabriel Dufan. Who's the other one?"

Dufan and his partner, hadn't yet seen them.

"Hey," Thunder yelled. "We help. Wait."

Gabriel looked up to see who it was. The two Chilkats had their parka hoods thrown back since it wasn't really cold at this low altitude. The big Canuck grinned wearily when Thunder and Lightning came up.

"Py gar," he said. "Dis one is about done." He sat down on the overturned sled. The dogs had already taken the opportunity to flop down in the snow. Gabriel's partner did likewise, throwing off his parka hood. They recognized Nunek, who had been Mama Borealis's husband. He grinned weakly. "Pooped too," he allowed, using English. He went to sleep practically on his feet, sagging over onto the sled.

Thunder stayed with the two exhausted men, sending Lightning back for help. "Bring Mo-gette, too," he ordered.

By dark they had the fagged-out pair down at Hedley's trading post, fed and in bed. Gabe managed to tell Dolf their story while getting a hot meal and half a bottle of whiskey down at Jack Quillen's cabin. In a nutshell, there had been too many prospectors attracted to St. John the previous season—and not enough food for the winter. The usual provision boats were caught by an early freeze hundreds of miles down the Yukon. Scurvy and smallpox were sweeping the interior.

When Maggie heard that, her heart felt like lead in her

breast. Their adopted daughter, little Maggie, was at the mercy of these dread killers at Elsie's and John Hedley's place in St. John. She thought, *I promised Mama Borealis I'd raise her daughter. Now look what's happened. Maybe the dear little girl, now two, was already dead and in an early grave, like her mother. If she is,* Maggie told herself, *I'm to blame. We could have brought her out with us.* But John and Elsie also loved the toddler and had no children of their own. They'd begged to keep her, so Dolf and Maggie had left her without much concern, knowing she was in loving hands. Dolf read his wife's thoughts on her face even as she implored him, "What can we do? Maggie may already be dead."

Dolf said, "I'm not sure. Maybe we can get some stuff at Juneau to vaccinate her, if I can get up there in time. I'll take a load of canned lemon juice up, too." He knew that was both a preventative and a cure for scurvy, even better than the cheaper lime juice used by the British navy.

Maggie hadn't considered the possibility that anyone might try to travel over Gabe's back trail with winter relentlessly closing in. It would get far colder than it was, the blizzards more severe. Hunting for game to feed the dog teams would also be uncertain—even assuming the pass could be negotiated in the first place.

"If you go, I go," she announced.

"Like hell!" he said.

She wasn't to be put off that easily, but she didn't press the point just then. She had an ace in the hole in that she was a skillful nurse with a great deal of training—and had once even helped save Dolf's life. She bided her time.

Dolf prepared a note to Sheriff Paul Brown in Juneau, explaining the emergency and requesting what they needed. He dispatched Thunder with the note in a large canoe similar to the one they'd come here in. After that, all they had to do was wait—and pray. Dolf was sure Brown would not tell anyone in Juneau where they were, even if Stan King got out a dozen warrants for each of them.

At first light the next morning they were awakened by Rafe Hedley pounding on their door. Dolf answered the knock in his nightshirt.

"Better get ready to haul yer freight somewhere," Rafe said without preamble. "the Navy's standin' off for high tide. They don't come up here for nothing."

"When's high tide?" Dolf asked.

"Mebbe two hours. They might put off a dinghy and walk in over the shingle before then, but if I know those fellers they won't."

Rafe had been told all about their recent Juneau misfortunes. He also knew of their previous plan to go and hide out at Billy Moore's place, a move which had been delayed by Gabe's arrival. Rafe's mind was as wily as his brother's and had been working rapidly. "I got an ice house up the river a ways. Why don't you an' Maggie hide out up there till they pull out? Got a lean-to on it. I'll roust out Knucks and git him up there, too. We can tell 'em you pulled out in that canoe with Thunder for gawd knows where. They might even have passed him on their way up. If they did they'll believe that fer sure. If they try to pump them Chilkats over in the village, they won't get the time of day."

By then Maggie was at the door behind Dolf, and overheard Rafe's spiel. Dolf shrugged. "I'd let 'em take us in, but we got business over yonder." He pointed toward the interior with his thumb.

Rafe, of course, knew what Dolf meant. He was heart-and-soul behind Dolf's plan to cross the mountains and take emergency supplies down the Yukon. Rafe Hedley and his crusty older brother had been exceptionally close since their orphaned youth. Old John's life was on the line, too.

"Uh. oh," he said, pushing Dolf inside. "Here comes trouble." Just before Rafe shut the door, Dolf saw four bluejackets with rifles in charge of an officer.

"We've got to get dressed quick," he told Maggie. "Navy crawling around out in the yard."

Rafe, who was well-known to all the Navy personnel in the area, went to head them off.

"Howdy, Mr. Jelly," he greeted the ensign in charge. "Howdy, boys. What brings you up this way?" He cursed the luck that had placed Jelly, a young Academy man, in charge of this detail. The kid had been bucking for admiral since the day he'd stepped out of Annapolis.

Jelly wore his best official mien, trying to look like a steel engraving of Admiral Farragut. "I'd bet you know why I'm here. Who was that I saw duck back in the cabin over there?"

"What'd they do?" Rafe asked, avoiding a direct answer.

"Depends on who they are," Jelly stated.

Rafe grinned. "They're the honeyockers I hired to farm this place. A dumb Swede and his wife. They didn't look very dangerous to me, but you never know."

Jelly said, "You sure they aren't Dolf Morgette and his wife? I got warrants for both of them." He pulled them out.

Rafe reached for them so he could look them over as a means to stall for more time. Meanwhile, Dolf and Maggie were frantically tossing on enough clothing to protect them if they had to run for it. Jim Too, sensing something amiss, barked once. Dolf quieted him.

"You seen Morgette?" Jelly asked Rafe.

Rafe eyed him levelly. "Yep. Seen him yestiddy. He and his whole crew pulled out in a big canoe."

Jelly remained unconvinced. He kept eying the Morgette cabin over Rafe's shoulder. "Where for?"

"He didn't say. Seemed in an all-fired hurry. Maybe back to Juneau."

Jelly shook his head. "Not likely. That's where these warrants came from. Him and his wife are both wanted down there."

"For what?"

"Murder and kidnapping."

"You don't say?" Rafe tried to look shocked. "What happened?" He was stalling for more time. Jelly sensed that.

He turned to his rifle squad and ordered, "You two go around back of that cabin." Not knowing the names, he pointed out to two men.

"Hold on a minute," Rafe growled. "I don't know as I cotton to you throwin' yer weight around here, doubtin' my word. You bastards got no more right than a jackrabbit to be servin' warrants, an' you know it."

Jelly paused. "That never seemed to bother you when you needed help keeping your Indians in line."

"That's a different story," Rafe countered. "That's your job. I happen to know there's a law against you fellers acting as a posse. I was a deputy sheriff once under my brother up in Montana. We went to the fort for some help and they told us to go to hell. Told us all about that law, too. That's what I'm tellin' you. If you wanta keep them pretty blue overalls and be an admiral someday, and not spend the next couple of years in court, you'd better tread soft. Baker and Hedley can pull wires in Washington."

The two seamen hadn't moved, waiting for the outcome of the argument, which all four were savoring since Jelly obviously wasn't winning it. Besides, they'd all been rolled at least once in the Skookum, and, like Blunderbuss Newgast, thought that if the Morgettes had killed Goldie they merited a medal.

Jelly was disturbed by the situation his superior, Lieutenant Beeman, had placed him in. He also supsected that the reason Beeman had side-stepped the honor of this job had been precisely what Rafe Hedley had just mentioned.

"Hedley," he said, "I'll accept your word of honor as a gentleman if you assure me Morgette and his wife are no longer here."

Rafe almost guffawed. He could hardly wait to write to Old John about being dubbed a gentleman by the U.S. Navy.

"Why, hell, yes," he said. "I already done that. I may be a leetle sharp in a business deal, but I don't lie for anybody." It sounded so convincing he almost believed it himself. He had neglected to add a small caveat: that he didn't lie for anybody *but his friends*.

"I'll accept that," Jelly said. He extended his hand and they shook on it. "All right, men," he ordered. "We'll get back aboard." He pointed to one of them. "You're in charge. I'll be down to the boat in a couple of minutes."

When they had marched well out of hearing the seaman in charge growled, "That son of a bitch has gone in for a drink."

Rafe saw that Jelly got several drinks while he sent someone down with a half pint for each of the seamen. The small, flat bottles could be concealed in a sock beneath bell-bottom trousers, as he well knew.

Rafe hadn't exactly lied either. By the time he gave his solemn word as a gentleman, Dolf and Maggie had slipped into the nearby brush, Jim Too following, and were all on their way to the icehouse. They, indeed, had left. More or less.

CHAPTER 15

THE growing relationship between Shiv Filetti and Nilda hadn't escaped Schoolboy Mumma. Grudgingly, he gave Shiv high marks for his enterprise. He, of course, had no idea that Nilda had been the prospector and Shiv the lode.

The thought that he might be in line to be shoved out of the picture had also occurred to him. He wasn't certain that it would make much difference, since the picture was unclear with Goldie dead. He wasn't aware that Nilda planned to go ahead with Goldie's scheme to heist the spring cleanup from the Sky Pilot. In any case, he planned to quietly pump Shiv on the situation. He was also considering how he might pair up with Lobo Lafferty against the other two—assuming Lobo would pull through, and in case Shiv and Nilda froze him out. Well, he told himself, Mrs. Mumma's little boy has always managed to get his share somehow.

He grinned, stretched out on one of the big chairs in the Skookum's clubroom where he and Shiv were still living, puffed on one of Goldie's perfectos, and sipped his good Kentucky straight. He thought, regardless of what happens, this sure beats a boil on my butt. Life had taught him to take things one day at a time. Today was pretty good. The previous two days had been even better. He'd been big winner in a couple of all-night poker sessions, and was a few thousand bucks richer as a result. He'd thought of heading back to Frisco and blowing his roll on a girl he knew there. That set him to thinking of Lizzie LaBelle right next door. He strolled out and tapped on her door.

At that moment, down in Nilda's apartment, the brokenhearted widow was in consultation with Filetti. Two days had passed since Goldie's burial. Nilda had thanked her lucky stars several times for her liberation. Moreover, not a soul had questioned her status as the widow and rightful heir. As she knew, she'd not only inherited Goldie's savings—a bankroll of some fifty thousand dollars in an account in San Francisco—but she was now fully in charge of the local gold mine known as the Skookum.

Hubie figured largely in her plans. In fact, if her bogus marriage certificate were ever questioned, she planned to marry him. Bigamy was no more an obstacle in her mind than the forgery that had placed her in the driver's seat. Chicago was a long ways off, and Hubie had confessed to her that he planned never to return there. He'd shown her a picture of his wife. She had taken one look and agreed he'd made a sound decision. At the time he'd said, "I'll kinda miss Jeff, though."

"Your kid?" she asked.

"My dog," he said. He had a picture of Jeff, too. She had to admit he beat the haycock wife for looks.

"Send for him," she had suggested.

Hubie was just then on his way down to the kitchen to float a loan in order to do just that. He could work to repay the loan, he figured. The only rub would be if his wife refused to ship the dog, and kept the express money for herself. He frowned at the thought as he padded down the hall in his stockinged feet. The sound of Filetti's voice in the kitchen made him halt. He realized that the killer liked him for some reason; nonetheless, he was afraid of Shiv. When able to make out what Shiv had said, he turned to go back to his room, but Nilda's reply came through clearly.

"We may not have to kill anyone if we do it my way."

Hubie's heart beat faster. He was afraid to be caught overhearing that kind of talk, but he was also anxious to find out who might be in line to be killed next. It was also a shock to hear sweet, innocent, blue-eyed Nilda talk in that manner. Her next words shook him even more. "I don't see any reason to put Morgette out of the way—except as a last resort."

Filetti laughed. "It'll be a last resort, all right; as far as I'm concerned. Look what happened to Lobo Lafferty."

Nilda said something Hubie couldn't make out, then added, "Are you afraid of him?"

"Damn right," was the reply. "But I can get him if the setup is right."

"Well, let's hope it doesn't come to that. If my plans for dear brother Hubie works out, it won't come to that."

Hubie's ears really pricked up at that information. She said something else he couldn't decipher.

Filetti responded, "What makes you think he'll do it?"

Nilda laughed. "He'll do it. He'll do whatever I tell him. You did."

It was Filetti's turn to laugh. He wasn't aware how far Nilda's relationship with Hubie had progressed. If he had been, he'd have been jealous.

"You'd sure as hell earn what you got," Shiv concluded.

Hubie was assailed by conflicting emotions. He hated to find that Nilda was the hard schemer she appeared to be, and was gripped by fear that he might be caught if he stayed to hear more—though he dearly wanted to. Further, he was developing an inner resolve to show her she couldn't put a ring in his nose.

Nilda said, "It'll work just about like I told you—wait and see. If I can get him a job with Baker and Hedley up at St. John, we can get our haul before it even gets on the boat for outside. Who'd suspect him? Beside, he told me the Morgettes took a shine to him. If Morgette puts in a good word for him, Hedley will hire him as bookkeeper in a minute."

"What makes you so sure the Morgettes will be up there after what happened?" Filetti asked. "King's got the law on 'em."

"If they aren't it won't make any difference. I'll still need you and the boys—probably Rudy Dwan and some others I know. They're up at St. Michael with the crew, building the fast boat I told you about. We'll just hijack the shipment the way Goldie planned in the first place."

This stunned Hubie. He'd been trying not to believe the worst about his older brother. He still had warm memories of their youth when Rupert had been the leader of the other boys. Now he wished he had someone to confide in. He wasn't well enough acquainted with the local law (such as it was) to trust either Newgast or Brown. He felt his mistrust was justified by the way the Morgettes had fared at their hands. He didn't believe for a moment that Margaret Morgette had killed his brother—yet she was now a fugitive based on a warrant issued by Newgast, which, as far as Hubie knew, Brown wouldn't hesitate to serve. He'd have confided in Margaret if he could, but he had no idea where she and Dolf were.

Then his mind turned to Lizzie LaBelle, a nice, warm-hearted girl. Maybe he could sound her out for some way to tackle his problem. He wasn't quite sure how, and he had no intention of spilling the beans till he was sure he could trust her. But she was a lot more wordly-wise than he was, and, moreover, the only person he knew in town aside from Nilda and the three killers. Besides, he had another reason for wanting to see Lizzie, though he was scarcely conscious of it. First, however, he had to get back to his room and make a noisy exit, this time with his shoes on.

His heart was in his mouth as he tiptoed back, praying the floor wouldn't creak and give him away. Once safely in his room, he gave himself a few minutes to settle down before putting on his shoes. Chicago was beginning to look good to him, only he lacked the return fare. He thought, What a hell of a mess to be in.

His main problem now was going to be acting natural around Nilda. He wondered what he'd do if she came to him as she had before. He figured he'd be scared to death, which would arouse her suspicions. He prayed that she wouldn't visit him, but he had experience enough to suspect the inducement by which she hoped to control him. He muttered under his breath, "What a pickle for a dumb guy like me to get into."

Then a sudden resolve flooded him. I'll be damned if I want to be back home, he told himself; I'd almost 'ruther die. He drew himself up to his full height, threw back his shoulders, banged his door open noisily, and thought, *here goes*. He walked past the kitchen and saw that Shiv had departed. Nilda was alone at the table nursing a coffee mug and staring blankly at the wall. He cleared his throat to get her attention. Her eyes focused on him as her mind returned from wherever it had been.

"I was just going out," he said.

She smiled sweetly, but it didn't strike him as it had before. He tried to see behind it to where the demon—capable of murder—lurked, but he saw nothing except what she wanted to project.

"Come in and sit down before you go out," she said. "I want to talk to you."

He did as commanded, unable not to, though he'd rather have run.

She didn't waste time sparring. "How well did you know Goldie?" she asked, though she knew the answer.

He gulped, suspecting what was coming. "Not very well, I guess," he admitted.

She nodded. "He was one of the biggest crooks that ever lived. I hated him. I'm glad he's dead."

She watched him closely for a reaction. He was stunned, as incapable as a small boy of coping with her brutal language. Yet a similar realization had been tugging at his mind.

She laughed at his open-mouthed reaction and placed her warm hand against his chubby cheek. "You're just a child, Hubie, and I love you for it."

As he'd feared, she was soon leading him to the slaughterhouse. She must think him as trusting as a worn-out dairy cow. He dreaded what was coming when she tugged him into her bedroom. He'd underestimated his woman. Skillfully she coaxed him into forgetting everything but her warm body beside him; demanding, yet yielding. Soon his head was again in shape for the attention of the woodpeckers.

Later she leaned over and blew her warm breath on his ear. "How'd you like to be a rich man, Hubie?" she whispered.

He didn't answer, didn't need to, couldn't. It seemed a great idea to him, especially if she were to continue inspiring him as she just had. Besides, he'd always had a normal desire to be rich.

Nilda knew what his answer was. She smiled. Hubie was soon in an exhausted sleep, flat on his back with his mouth open, starting to snore. She looked him over, not without genuine affection, and again concluded there was a lot to fat, little, cherubic Hubie. Smiling, she closed the door quietly and slipped away.

CHAPTER 16

RAFE Hedley watched the Navy ship weigh anchor, periodically re-checking its position until it was only a speck under a plume of black smoke. Then it vanished far down the canal. He was sure its departure wasn't merely a ruse to lure the Morgettes from hiding.

Rafe walked back to the icehouse. He approached cautiously, yelling until he heard Dolf's answer before entering. He suspected that there would have been four dead sailors and an ensign if the Navy men had forced their way into the cabin.

"All clear," he yelled after Dolf answered his hail.

On the way back to the trading post he volunteered, "I allow it'd be safer if you folks sloped over to Billy Moore's place tonight. I'll go with you."

"I kinda had the same notion," Dolf said. "We'll start gettin' our possibles together and head out after dark. We'll want a lot of truck and about four dog teams. I figure to be set in case we get snowed in, makin' it down the Yukon to St. John this time o' year."

"I admire yer guts. Can't say as I'd care to try it. Especially over Chilkoot Pass. But Gabe made it in, so I guess you can do it, too," Rafe said.

"Thunder says there's a better way over behind Billy Moore's," Dolf told him. "You don't have to go as high, and the snow's lighter."

Rafe laughed. "I'll bet. Prob'ly only seventy foot instead of eighty or ninety. But the Injuns does it when they have to, I reckon."

Dolf said, "Can't let a leetle snow stop us. I been up there three winters, and I'll say this for it—if yuh wait for good weather to travel you'll make about ten miles a month. I aim to make that much on bad days and sixty on good ones."

Rafe started to say If yer damn lucky, then thought better of it. Chances favored being snowed in about half the time by blinding blizzards. When the snow let up the arctic winds blew. Sometimes the mercury froze in the tube at seventy below, and walking outside could cause frostbite of the lungs of man or beast.

By then they were back at the Morgettes' cabin. Margaret spoke for the first time. "Come on in. I'll get a good breakfast for us. Coffee was on when we left. The Hummingbird probably saw that it didn't boil away." In fact, the aroma of coffee hit their nostrils as they entered the warm cabin.

Seeing Rafe hesitate, Dolf said, "C'mon in. I want you to help me make out a list. It'll be a long one. What we can't run over to Moore's with us today, I'd like you to send over as soon as you can."

"Suits me," said Rafe. He and Dolf were soon at the kitchen table working out a list while Maggie got breakfast started.

"First of all is good bedrolls," Dolf said. "We want wolf-skin bags for everybody and a pair of Hudson's Bay blankets apiece. I found out the hard way that a man better just dig in in the snow and sleep, when it's too cold to move. We'll need some saws and shovels to build snow holes. And whisk brooms to keep the powder snow out of our clothes and bags. If that powdery snow melts and freezes in your duds, you might as well be wrapped in mosquito net as in furs and blankets."

Rafe nodded, writing the list as Dolf dictated.

They stopped when Maggie served breakfast, then resumed over coffee. By the time they had finished the list ran to several pages, and included everything from dark glasses to ward off snow blindness to ammunition for hunting. Dolf had learned the wisdom of carrying both a .22 and a shotgun in addition to his .45-90 Winchester. The former was good for shooting rabbit, the latter for birds. Dolf also used his .22 on ptarmigan, which were a good deal like the fool hens back home that were too incautious to fly. The .22 ammunition was lighter to pack. Their food list carried many items of dried foods which were lighter and more compact than canned goods. A large part of the load would have to consist of dried fish for the dogs. Of course, if the hunting were good (which was sometimes not the case, for reasons no one understood), feeding the humans and dogs would be no problem. Caribou and moose were large animals. The dogs would consume all the normally unused meat and bones without leaving a scrap.

By the time their list was completed, Gabriel Dufan had strolled in, followed by Nunek. The latter held back, unused to a welcome from whites. "C'mon," Gabriel had urged. "My fren Morgette's got an Injun wife himself." Nunek was still hesitant. Maggie went over and greeted him, taking his hand and leading him to the table. "Sit down, both of you," she invited. "I'll put some more breakfast on."

Nunek grinned his thanks, looking over the Hummingbird with interest while drinking a cup of coffee he had filled with a quarter cup of sugar. The Hummingbird pretended not to notice his attention. No one had told her as yet that this had been her sister's husband. Too much else had been going on.

Dolf addressed Gabe. "I want to go over our list of stuff to take to the interior." Gabe read it through. "What do you think?" Dolf asked. "Did we forget anything?"

Gabe grinned. "Too tam much flour, not enough firewater."

Dolf noticed that Gabe's English had improved since he'd first known him. He'd taken to such expressions as "firewater" for "whiskey"—no doubt because they appealed to his sense of humor. Dolf was glad to see that the big Métis hadn't suffered too much from his ordeal—had perhaps lost a little weight, but not much. Gabe normally scaled in at two thirty-five or so—which on a six-foot frame made him broad and solid. His hair was still coal black though he was pushing forty and had had a hard outdoor life, and his beard and mustache were the same shiny color. Best of all, however, was the usual sparkle in his wideset dark eyes. They gleamed out at the world from deep sockets which framed a hooked, pirate's nose. When he laughed, which was often, he showed a perfect set of long, white teeth.

He laughed just then as Knucks, looking a trifle worse from a night with the bottle, joined the gathering. "Poy," Gabe snorted. "Dem eyeballs look lak cherries."

Knucks appraised him solemnly. "That sleepin' medicine we gave you didn't exactly do anything fer yers either, pal. You looked in a mirror this morning?"

"Every mornin'," Gabe said. "I admire me."

Everyone was grinning at this exchange. "Man, you need glasses," Knucks retorted.

"What for?" Gabe asked. "I can't read."

Knucks feigned disgust. "I'll tell you someday. I can see it'll take awhile to get it in that thick French head o' yours."

Maggie plopped down three plates for the new arrivals. "Hush all of you. You're fogging up the room," she said. They ignored her.

"I'm gonna mosey over to the store with Rafe and get started on our outfit," Dolf announced. He was weighed down with the thought that what they carried with them would be the sole basis of their success or failure on a hazardous journey—that and luck. There would be eight of them, two to a sled. He planned to use only five dogs to a sled, with Jim Too as lead dog on one of them. He'd learned that his big dog would play second fiddle to none, and had whipped bigger dogs to make his point.

His smaller-sized teams (seven or eight were common), Dolf balanced off against the lesser amount of food that would be needed. He had two women on his hands, which was a worry, though he knew Maggie could hold her own, in addition to helping break trail or push on a sled. He didn't know about the Hummingbird. She'd been around the settlements and might not be in shape for the trail.

Maggie had shrugged that off. "Wait and see," she'd argued. "Her kind are tough. I have a hunch we'll be glad we brought her." The others would be himself, Knucks, Thunder and Lightning, Gabe and Nunek. A substantial part of their load would be in the canned lemon extract he'd sent Thunder to Juneau for. At least none of his party would get scurvy—though there was the risk of starving if their luck ran out. Dolf prayed that Doc Meadows had a supply of smallpox vaccine. Like Maggie, he loved their adopted daughter—just as they both loved Henry. It wasn't a matter of blood but the bond of familiarity that counted. The dusky, beady-eyed little infant had captured all their hearts, including that of crusty Old John Hedley and his Sioux wife Elsie. Consciousness of the importance of speed made him anxious, though he knew that undue haste could result in (equally fatal) poor planning.

After a busy day of preparation, they shoved off with a heavily laden canoe. It was well toward midnight, and they kept a wary eye out for some sign of the Navy slipping back in on them. The sleds and dogs—except for Jim Too—would be carried on a separate trip. The water in the canal was smooth as glass. It was, however, subject to the caprices of arctic weather. A wind could whip it up with little warning. Thus, they stayed close to shore, working their way along the mountains that fell into the water, usually at a sixty-degree angle. There were breaks in the cliffs where they could beach in an emergency—provided they were close enough when the need arose.

Bill Moore had chosen a spot—Skagway—which was to become famous in another decade. For ten years he would develop his farm, only to see his stake jumped by thousands of gold-mad stampeders—his claims ignored by everyone, even the government. (But that was years off, as was his re-markable response: of turning the stampede into a personal bonanza by building the docks on which freight through Skagway had to be loaded or unloaded.)

The name "Skagway" was taken from the Indian word for "a windy place." This night Dolf's party were lucky, landing just at first light with the water calm as a lily pond.

CHAPTER 17

DURING the three nights that the Morgette party stayed with Billy Moore, Margaret had a recurring dream. Somehow she and Dolf were alone in an empty expanse of snow. A hurricane wind was blowing, tearing up long streamers of granulated snow and driving them erratically across a crusty surface. The wind snatched her breath away as—cold and desperately weary—she struggled to stay on her feet. Only a short distance ahead, Dolf was beckoning her to cross the last few feet to what she knew was safety. But from what she wasn't certain, nor did she know why he wouldn't (or couldn't) come help her. Complete panic and desperation gripped her. She looked behind to see if she were being pursued, but she saw nothing but the vast panorama of snowy wilderness that sloped down to a dark blue arm of the sea. Alabaster mountains rose beyond it.

When she turned back, a strong gust of wind clouded the air with a dense mass of snow, obscuring Dolf from her vision. Then the wind abated, the snow cloud evaporated, but Dolf had vanished. She turned completely around. Nothing was in sight except the endless, sparkling depth of the blue sky above a field of blinding white. Even the ocean had disappeared. A single black raven drifted silently over her, floating downwind until it was gone. The wind died. Everything was pervaded by a deathly stillness.

"Dolf," she called. "Where are you?" Not even an echo was returned. She called louder—as loud as she could, "Dolf!" Then from nowhere he came and was holding her close, and she knew it was really him, that she'd been having a nightmare but was now safe in the sleeping bag beside him in the soft hay in Moore's stable.

"You were dreaming, honey," he said softly.

"I know," she said.

"What?"

"Just a silly dream," she murmured, already half-asleep again. The last thing she remembered was him holding her tightly.

In the morning, the details of the dream passed through her mind, troubling the part of her that was still Indian. Maybe her father or the shaman Strong Bull could have interpreted the dream for her. They both believed that dreams often foretold coming events. She thought, if this one does, I must be going to get lost in the snow. She wasn't sure she could put full stock in what she half-believed might be nothing more than superstition.

When Billy Moore heard that Cap had sent them he said, "If that old fossil swears by yuh, I reckon yore okay by Billy Moore." To Rafe Hedley he tossed the greeting, "What brings you here, you crooked old bastard?"

It didn't ruffle Rafe, though Billy said it with a straight face. Everybody else quickly realized they were old friends. Rafe replied, "Come to see that you ain't drunk yerself to death yet."

Billy grunted. "Fat chance. I give it up. Even run off my klootch."

"Haw," Rafe laughed. "When you give up on hootch and chickens I'll be lookin' fer another star of Bethlehem."

Everyone understood that "klootch" was native for "squaw," as was "chicken." "Hootch" originally referred to Hootchinoo—the Indians' potent brew—a name shortened by the sourdoughs and applied to all hard liquor.

That day, the sleds and dog teams arrived from Dyea, in a second big cargo canoe, along with additional supplies. The following day Thunder arrived with provisions from Juneau, the most important of which was an airtight jar containing twenty quills impregnated with smallpox vaccine. Doc Meadows had sent a note with it:

"Can't guarantee any of these will work, but if they do there's less danger using this than vaccinating from someone that has smallpox. If it don't work, you'll have to try the other way as a last resort."

He included instructions for how to vaccinate—either from the material he'd sent or from the infectious pustules of someone suffering from an active case of smallpox.

Margaret took charge of the vaccine. She explained the note to Dolf. "What he means is, better hope the vaccine is still potent. The other way, people sometimes die just like they do when they catch the disease."

Dolf prayed that the vaccine would work. He asked Maggie, "Why wouldn't it work?"

She shrugged. "Maybe too old. Who knows? Sometimes it doesn't, that's all."

"It'll work," Dolf said positively. "A hunch."

"I hope so," she said. She almost asked if he had any hunches about whether they'd get there in time to protect their daughter, then held her tongue. He had enough to worry him.

At first light the following day they started the four dog teams. It was an unusual, clear day, perfect for a start. To the east, snow-clad slopes were tinted pink by the rising sun. Above that the sky was almost purple, turning to a strange, opaque white overhead, and remaining a deep, midnight blue in the west. It shimmered as though it were made of minute crystals.

After climbing through belts of willow brush and spruce, the sleds topped out on the bare slope of a ridge some five hundred feet above their starting point. Dolf and Margaret were on the last sled, he leading, she on the gee pole. Margaret looked back and caught her breath, her heart pounding rapidly. Before her lay the very scene from her dream—a deep, cold, blue sea churned by angry whitecaps, the shimmering white mountains beyond, all bathed in the first rays of the sun. She turned her head upward, expecting to see the raven as it drifted past. She felt faint. Should she tell Dolf about the dream, she wondered? He'd probably laugh at her. They soon moved on, but she was dogged by leaden depression, sure that disaster lurked ahead.

Soon, the mackerel sky foretold a change. Behind them, to the west, a tall bank of clouds reached halfway to the zenith. The mountains were capped by telltale plumes of snow hurled horizontally by high winds. When they stopped for a noon snack and rest, Gabriel Dufan scanned the sky and observed, "Big snow on the way."

Thunder nodded, pointing west. He said, "Mebbe so lotsa snow. Dat many day sometimes." He held up the fingers of both hands.

"Think we can travel in it?" Dolf asked.

Thunder looked at the sky again and shrugged. "Prolly," he said. Then, "Mebbe not. Specially dis side." He pointed east. "Dat side mo' betta."

Dolf felt a sense of urgency to get under way. He wasn't the type to get stalled because he'd moved too slowly. "Okay, everybody," he ordered. "Let's get going."

The first snowflakes dropped from the leaden sky at dusk, which at that season was about three-thirty. The wind then threw out exploratory fingers, causing an immediate added chill in the air. "We'll keep movin' as long as we can see, unless the dogs tire out," Dolf ordered at their next brief stop. He'd been altering lead sleds so that the burden of breaking trail was equally divided. He'd kept a wary eye on the Hummingbird, who was paired on a sled with Nunek. He was surprised, and glad, to see that she seemed to be doing as well as any of them. He himself was feeling the strain of the trail after several months away from it, though he'd started Maggie and himself jogging as soon as he knew they'd be heading north by dog sled. They had had less than a week of conditioning—not enough by far. He knew they'd be stiff that night, and stiffer still in the morning.

By full dark the blizzard struck with brutal force, blanking out visibility beyond fifty feet. They halted in a spruce thicket beneath a sheltering cliff. There, the snow fell nearly straight down, rapidly accumulating on everything.

"I reckon we can make out under canvas here," Dolf guessed. He parceled the work out among the party: the women cooking; he, Knucks and Gabe gathering wood; the three Indian men feeding the dogs. After eating, they followed the example of the dogs, bundling up in their robes with a tarp below and over them. The dogs curled into an almost perfect ball, nose to tail, as they lay in the shelter of the rock wall. They could survive that way even in the open, beneath their heavy winter coats, to temperatures of sixty degrees below—or even lower. Jim Too was having a harder time of it, not having been up North during the early fall. During the night he nudged Dolf under his tarp. Dolf awoke, figured out the dog's problem, and lifted the tarp—which was now heavily burdened with snow. The big dog crept in next to him, sheltered at least from the wind. "Derned if yer gettin' inside with me and Maggie, though," he said. Jim Too licked his face, then curled up with a huge sigh of contentment. Dolf pulled his head back under their robe and was asleep again almost immediately.

The following morning the snow was heavier than it had been the night before. It was necessary to burrow out and pull everything from under the blanket of snow. "Musta got a least eighteen inches," Dolf told Maggie when he stuck his head outside. He got out of the robe carefully so as not to get any snow on him. Dressing was no problem, since the only clothing anyone with sense in that country ever removed at night was his parka and fur cap, or, if he had to change into dry socks, his mukluks. Like house dogs, experienced Arctic travelers also learned to condition themselves to infrequent calls of nature. Most of it was a case of life at the most rudimentary level of survival. People became either tough, wise survivors—or corpses. Everybody present—with the possible exception of the Hummingbird—had already proved themselves to be survivors, even under the worst conditions. Knucks had only one prior winter under his belt, but he had spent it running a long trapline under the tutelage of the wilderness-wise Gabriel Dufan.

Dolf impatiently appraised the dense clouds of snow which restricted visibility to a stone's throw at the best of times, and during heavy gusts of wind to zero. Suspecting what the answer would be, he nonetheless called his three Indian men together to ask what the chances were of traveling in such weather. The others, looking to Thunder as their natural leader, waited for him to answer first. He didn't hesitate. "No good. Mebbe fall in big hole." He meant off a cliff. The others nodded, faces serious. "Yah," Lightning agreed. "Break neck mebbe. Like dat." He made a motion for breaking a stick over his knee. Nunek was silent, nodding agreement.

The snow continued to fall at a rate that threatened to bury them. By the next evening, an additional three feet had fallen. Still, there was no sign of it slacking off. They had to continually raise the canvas under which the women had their cooking fire to keep off the snow. They sat in its shelter, occasionally going out for wood. Dolf shook his head, conscious of the possible consequences of delay. He was tired of sitting around with the men: smoking, draining the coffee pot, swapping lies. He got up and looked at the sky, able to see only a blinding swirl of snow.

"Hell, at this rate we could be here all winter," he grumbled. He kicked at the woodpile. Sensing his dark mood and the reason for it, no one spoke. "I think I'll roll in and get some shut-eye," he said.

Margaret had already taken that practical approach to the necessity of doing nothing. The dogs hadn't moved all day, patiently waiting for their rations to break the monotony. Jim Too was still under the tarpaulin, grudgingly moving over to make room for Dolf. Following Dolf's lead, the rest turned in after dragging in the next day's supply of dry, deadfall wood.

A second day passed as the first—without a break in the blizzard. Maggie could read the effect of the enforced delay on Dolf. She knew him to be remarkably patient, a trait honed during his five years in prison, but back then no one's life had depended upon him getting out.

At suppertime on the second day Dolf said, "If the weather doesn't break pretty soon, I'm gonna risk it alone. You can follow me when it breaks up."

"Too tam risky, I tink," Gabe said. "But if you go, I go wit you, my fren."

"I'll go with him," Maggie protested.

Knucks broke in. "How about we all go? I don't expect to live forever, and I sure don't aim to go from bein' bored outa my gourd." He looked around at the group. "How about you?" he asked the three Indian men.

"Suits me," Thunder said. He spoke for the other two. "Where Moh-gette go, Tunda go." He looked up at the sky. "Mebbe so tomorra betta, I tink."

He was a weather prophet. The next morning dawned crystal clear and cuttingly cold, the world glistening in the sun's rays that slanted through snow-draped spruce. Chickadees and gray juncos were on patrol, hopping in circles, often upside down on branches, beady eyes fixed on the camp as they waited to pounce on any abandoned edibles.

Maggie was as elated at the prospect of moving as Dolf. She had suffered both his feeling of desperate urgency and his painful frustration.

"How long to the other side?" Dolf asked Thunder.

The Chilkat held up two fingers. "Two day. 'Less it snow again."

"Will it?"

"Mebbe so." He shrugged eloquently.

Dolf knew it was a good possibility. He decided to press on, whether it snowed or not.

CHAPTER 18

GOOD weather (if that's what you could call twenty degrees below zero, with a cutting wind) saw the Morgette party over the crest that would later become known as the "White Pass." They camped on the far side, in a spot where there was shelter from the wind and good dry wood. The latter was plentiful due to deadfalls caused by the freakish, hurricane-force Arctic winds which sometimes blew down whole stands of trees in a swath. These fell entangled, interwoven like a randomly strewn bunch of matchsticks. Many were still above the snow. This was fortunate for the travelers, since by late winter one might sometimes have to burrow for wood under seventy feet of snow.

The day had been painfully bright. Everyone wore dark goggles, even the Indians who had taken enthusiastically to this convenient substitute for using soot to blacken their eye sockets and lids. Visibility was well over a hundred miles; they could see high mountains thrust skyward around the entire horizon.

They pushed on long after dark, provided with excellent visibility from the moon, which at that time of year circled low on the horizon. Even without moonlight, the light for the brightly winking stars reflected on the snow would have provided good visibility. As they were making camp with the thermometer falling rapidly, the northern lights gave a spectacular show. They rippled across every quadrant of the sky; sometimes pure white, sometimes red, pink, green, yellow, or a combination of the above, alternating between vast, sinuous rivers of luminosity and fields of shimmering color.

Margaret took a moment to marvel at them, as she always

would unless a matter of life and death were at hand. Later, after they had eaten and were wrapped warmly in their robes, she poked her head out for a final look at the sky. Clouds scudded overhead, foretelling another storm.

By morning there was another blizzard like the one that had blocked their ascent from the shore. This time they decided to dig in to ensure better shelter from the snow.

The men dug two circular holes about ten feet in diameter, joining them with a passage, and cutting exit holes from each. Over these they put stout branches brought to a peak like the poles of a teepee, though not as steeply slanted. These they covered with tarpaulin, tucking the base in a trench and anchoring it with packed snow, with an air hole at the top. Before putting on the tarpaulin, they dug small tunnels that radiated from the walls of the main holes. These were well below the surface, and were just large enough to accommodate their sleeping bags. This was done in a couple of hours, during which the falling snow threatened to cover the excavations as quickly as they were cleared. In new snow this shelter would have been impossible, but here the snow had been packed by several weeks' accumulation; alternate thawing and freezing had solidified it. It could actually be cut into blocks with saws, a fact that greatly facilitated the work. The blocks were then used to make shelters for the dogs.

This kind of camp was not new to Maggie, since she'd run Dolf's trapline with him several times in prior years. These snow holes, however, were larger than these they'd made for just the two of them.

"Jist like home," Knucks said, after they'd applied the final touches and were sitting inside by candlelight. "Almost, that is."

Huddled together in one of the rooms, Dolf, Maggie, Knucks, and Gabriel knew they were imprisoned—though not for long. The natives had rolled pragmatically into their holes in their apartment, recognizing that there was no defense against hours—perhaps days—of enforced idleness.

Except for Nunek (who was little Maggie's father), they were untouched by the sense of dire urgency that pressed on Maggie and Dolf.

Margaret had observed the frustrated tightening and relaxing of Dolf's jaw muscles and realized she was doing the same thing. Periodically, Dolf made his way to the exit by the flickering candlelight, cleared away the newly accumulated snow, and went out to check the weather.

"Still coming down," he'd say, resignedly. Such blizzards had been known to last for weeks. Maggie wondered what desperate things Dolf might risk if that happened. A fire, which would have cheered up their burrow, was confined to minimal cooking needs. Too much heat would cause the walls to sweat, then freeze, which would stop the natural ability of the snow to breathe—and threaten them all with suffocation. Knowledge both of this—and the need to keep the top vent from drifting shut—was one of the priceless lessons that the sourdoughs had learned from the natives. After each cooking fire, they carefully scraped the walls of any ice slick, using specially fashioned sections from a ripsaw. They saved the ice residue in a bucket to melt for drinking water at the next meal. Surprisingly, a single candle and their body heat provided a great deal of warmth in their confined quarters.

By the third day of confinement, Maggie was acquiring the native knack of sleeping most of the time. But it was not comfortable sleep: much of the time she was racking her mind for ways to escape their imprisonment. She wondered why they couldn't grope their way onward, with someone ahead to probe the path with a long pole, perhaps tied to the rest by a safety rope. Maybe if they got a ways further east, perhaps to Lake Bennett, the blizzard would be less intense, due to the lower altitude and the shelter of the mountains. She thought of proposing such a move to Dolf, whose comforting warmth was next to her. He often shifted and groaned, and she wondered if he, too, was half-awake. Yet she hesitated to speak for fear of waking him. She recognized that if her plan was feasible, he'd have thought of it and put it into effect long before. The act was, they were helplessly trapped by forces vastly more powerful than they. The fate of Little Maggie and their friends in St. John was in the hands of God. So she prayed again, fervently, and felt a little better.

Their confinement could have been intolerable if any of them had had the mean, sulky nature that sometimes led partners with cabin fever to fighting and murder. Luckily, none of them did. In fact, they all tried to entertain each other. Gabriel told them the full history of his almost personal war against Canada in the Métis Rebellion. He and Dolf reminisced over their mutual attempt, following that event, to rescue Gabe's friend LeMoine from the gallows. At the recollection of their failure, Gabe's emotions overcame him.

Knucks and Dolf spoke about their long years in the Idaho penitentiary where Knucks had taught Dolf to box and wrestle. Finally, there was a wedding—more or less. Nunek and the Hummingbird began sharing their sleeping arrangements.

Maggie was a trifle piqued. Privately she asked Dolf, "Didn't Nunek get another wife when Mama Borealis died?"

Dolf shrugged. "Maybe two. Who knows? They have their own way of doing things. At least they both look happier than they did."

That made sense. She remembered she'd been desperately unhappy in this country only during her months of enforced separation from Dolf. The Arctic depressed a great many people during the months of cold, bleak darkness. Some committed suicide, some went mad. But come to think of it, all of these had been single men; none were natives, none women. She thanked God the men in their bleak prison were not of that weak kind.

Seven days passed, broken by the small chores of cooking,

disposing of waste, feeding the dogs, extending the exit tunnels as they were buried in the drifting snow, keeping open the air vent (which itself became a tunnel), checking the weather, and—best of all—the blissful intervals of truly sound sleep.

Maggie was enjoying one of these when a shout startled her awake.

"Yahoo! The sun's out!" It was Knucks. "Wake up, all you hibernatin' bears."

She could hardly believe the day had come, having suffered like a kid waiting for Christmas. She felt at least as happy as such a kid on Christmas morning, as she pitched in with the men to get the sleds and harnesses free of snow and to recover the roof tarpaulins, which by then were under twenty feet of fresh snow. The dogs celebrated with a fight which required all hands to help break it up.

Dolf was obsessed with his sense of urgency, working without letup to get the outfit in shape to press on. Inevitably, it took hours.

He took the lead, breaking trail on his snowshoes at a constant trot, forcing the others to his pace. After a while he removed his parka to prevent sweating, which would lead to pneumonia after a sudden cooling-off.

"Hey, Dolf," Gabe finally yelled from his place on the next sled. "You tryin' ta keel your frens?"

Only then did Dolf slacken his pace, then stop. He didn't even feel tired, having gotten his second wind. He knew he could have kept up that pace all day, but he realized that, except for Maggie and Nunek, the others weren't obsessed with his urgency. He grinned at her. "How're you doin'?"

"Fine," she said, between gasps for breath. "I think." She had been sustained by the same urge that was driving him. Still, she knew she needed to rest, being near the limit of her endurance. Dolf read the weariness in her drawn face.

"We'll stop and make some tea and eat something," he announced.

After a rest she felt her strength returning. Due to Dolf's constant pace and a long day of mostly downhill travel, they reached the head of Lake Bennett before camping again.

The weather held. Travel on the frozen lakes and rivers relieved the burden of struggling uphill or pushing through heavy brush and timber. Maggie's spirits were high; the memory of her terrible nightmare had almost faded. They passed the spot on Lake Bennett where they had camped for weeks in '86, building their boats and waiting for the ice to break up. Dolf stopped the cavalcade there for a breather and lunch.

While they were eating, Dolf had been scanning the sky for signs of brewing weather. The first faint feathers of mackerel clouds were visible high over the mountains to the west.

"Best hit the trail again," he said.

It began to snow that night, but gently, so traveling was still possible. They moved down Tagish and Marsh Lakes through intermittent snow, finally approaching Miles Canyon, where Skookum Doc Hennessey had converted the bad Injun—Hoonah Charlie—into a good Injun with laughing gas and the painless extraction of an abcessed tooth. He'd been helped by some good whiskey, a set of false teeth, and his toupee. Hoonah Charlie and his murderous following were understandably awed by their first exposure to removable teeth and hair.

Dolf's party stopped now to parley before entering Miles Canyon.

Dolf said, "There could be open leads in there. Rough going at any rate, I'd bet, over the rapids."

He looked at the sky, which was still obscured by the snow that drifted steadily down through the still air. "We could go through without the sleds and check it, but I hate to waste any time. Can never tell when another real snow dumper'll hit us. I think we'll just go around." He turned to the Indian men for their opinion.

In this case, Nunek, who was more familiar with the interior, was the principal advisor. He said, "I tink dat betta. Mebbe so go bye-bye undah ice down dere." He pointed down the canyon.

So they elected the trail around the canyon. Dolf's fear of heavier snow was well-founded. Bringing up the rear, he and Margaret were often out of sight of Gabe's sled immediately ahead. Later they almost ran into it since Nunek, who was leading, had halted the cavalcade to come back and confer.

To Dolf he offered the opinion, "I tink betta camp here."

Dolf was familiar with the area and knew they were on top of the cliffs west of the river. He looked around. The trees nearby were still visible except when the growing gusts of wind swirled the ground snow into the sky. He was still goaded by a sense of urgency, augmented by the memory of their recent imprisonment. There were still hundreds of miles to go, and they'd found no game to increase their dwindling supply of dog food. A picture of little Maggie's sunny, gap-toothed grin played in his memory. It was the kind of situation in which all of his past experience had conditioned him to gamble.

"Go ahead awhile, but be careful. If we get snowed in again, it'll be a lot better at the foot of the canyon."

Nunek looked doubtful for a moment, then shrugged. "Hokay," he agreed, turning back to his team.

Maggie, handling the gee pole, saw that they were sometimes veering close to the cliffs. She wasn't too concerned. That was where the most open traveling was, where they'd portaged their supplies in '86. When the wind let up, the visibility was tolerable. During heavy gusts, she squinted her eyes almost shut and hung onto the sled. Thus, she had no warning when a twist of the sled angled her over the edge. She had no time to shout for help before her head struck a rock and she blacked out. Dolf, unaware that she was gone, pressed on along the soon-obscured trail, his eyes intent only on not losing it.

CHAPTER 19

DESPITE taking a chance trying to reach the foot of Miles Canyon in a blinding blizzard, Dolf was as prudent as circumstances permitted. For example, he frequently glanced behind him to assure himself that Maggie was still with him and that she was all right. To fail to do so would have been stupid and rash—and he was neither. In fact, in his voluminous reading of novels, he'd often deplored characters whom the author had made both stupid and rash in order to achieve dramatic effects. He'd often told himself, "If Natty Bumppo (or someone) wasn't a dunce, this book wouldn't have got by chapter one."

Therefore, it wasn't long before he discovered that Maggie wasn't with him. He stopped the team and shouted for the others to stop.

Gabe and Knucks were the first to reach him. "What's up?" Knucks asked.

"Maggie's gone." He couldn't bring himself to voice his suspicions of how or why. They all knew the cavalcade had several times passed perilously close to the canyon's palisades.

"How long?" Knucks asked.

"Not long. Less'n a minute. Set up camp here." He went forward and took Jim Too out of harness. As he did, Thunder and the others straggled back. "You and Lightning come with me," he told Thunder. "The rest of you set up camp." To Jim Too he said, "C'mon. Find Maggie."

They started back along the rapidly fading trail. If they moved quickly enough, he knew it would be no problem to find where Maggie had left them. She hadn't needed snowshoes, trotting in the rear position on a well-packed trail. The gee pole station seldom required snowshoes, except in very deep snow. The person there could also ride the back of the runners for a breather, as long as he wasn't on snowshoes. It would be easy to tell where her mukluk tracks stopped. Thunder took the lead, Jim Too right behind him. They found where she'd gone over in less than a minute.

Dolf shouted at the top of his voice, "Maggie! Maggie! Can you hear me?"

They waited in the funereal silence for an answering cry, but there was none—only the hiss of heavy snow falling on trees and bushes when the wind abated.

"All yell together," Dolf ordered. They set the canyon ringing with several cries in unison but received no response. "Get a long rope," Dolf told Lightning. "I'm going over the edge."

He waited where the skid mark of Maggie's fall was still plain. Peering down, he was occasionally able to see the river. He searched it anxiously for signs of open water where the swift current had resisted freezing up. There were none. He sighed, relieved on that count, but fidgeting at what seemed a long wait for the rope. Finally, Lightning returned with two long coils which they joined a rope long enough to reach the bottom one hundred feet below. Dolf secured one end to a large spruce, then let himself over the brink, descending hand over hand. He carefully scanned every seam in the cliff, every shelf that could have arrested her fall. About halfway down, the drop became sheer. He peered down to see if her crumpled body lay on the rocks below. If she'd taken that sheer drop, she'd be dead or critically injured. He cursed himself for not having taken Nunek's earlier advice to stop. Never in his life had he been so anxious, even when threatened with death himself. How the hell am I going to live without her? he wondered.

Then his feet touched bottom. Still keeping his hold on the rope he searched up and down from where she must have landed, but could see neither her nor any spot in the snow disturbed by her impact. At the very edge he pushed aside the snow-laden branches of a red willow. Beneath, the ice was dark. He tested it with his foot and was nearly pulled into an airhole, saved only by his grip on the rope. Alarmed, he drew back to examine the top of the bush for evidence that Maggie had fallen through it and gone beneath the ice. A great fear almost choked him. The clinging snow indeed seemed thinner where the bush met the sheer rock face. "I might have caused that myself," he argued, trying to retain a shred of hope even at the cost of self-deception.

He let out a huge sigh, looked bleakly upward, then turned to scan the river's frozen surface. Was his main reason for living somewhere far downstream, beneath the ice? This was only a short way from where she'd dived into the icy Yukon in '86 to save him and their infant son. What irony if she now died here, her skill as a swimmer useless in water so cold that one couldn't draw breath when immersed in it.

For an instant he felt like throwing himself down the open hole after her. All that restrained him was his knowledge that two children would now depend solely on him. That—and a thin thread of hope, no matter how flimsy.

"I don't see her anywhere," he yelled to those above. "I'm coming up." He worked hand over hand, walking his feet up the cliff, his body almost horizontal, It reminded him of scaling up the eerie black mine shaft in which he'd been trapped earlier that year in Pinebluff. He'd rather have been back there this minute, in peril of death himself, but certain that Maggie was still alive. He peered all about him on the way up, praying that perhaps he'd see Maggie from this new viewpoint, unconscious, her fall arrested by bushes or some irregularity in the rock wall.

On top again, his face told the story. It was bleak and

white. "Nothing," he said to the two Chilkats. "She's gone, I think, Open water in one place right down below."

Both looked as stricken as Dolf. "Too bad dat," Thunder said for both of them. "Mebbe so Tunda go look." He was too considerate to suggest openly that his eyes were better than Dolf's.

Dolf shrugged. "Why not?" It was a hope. Leadenly, he watched the Chilkat retrace his own recent course down the rope.

Maggie could remember having seen stars and pinwheels, then nothing. She was unconscious only briefly, then opened her eyes, blood flooding her head. She hung down, held by a foot caught in the densely entwined roots of a bush. Below was the hundred foot drop to the river. It almost erased her resolve to fight back up the cliff. One wrong move, she knew, and she would be dead. But days of running had hardened her muscles. She saved herself by a vertical sit-up. Once her head was closer to her trapped foot, she clambered into the bush using her hands. After freeing herself, she stopped for breath.

She felt as though she might pass out again. She was now on a small ledge. Her actions may have taken half a minute, then oblivion again enveloped her. This time her unconscious world filled with life and sound. An unfamiliar universe unfolded. She seemed to be lying on her back, eyes closed. Just before she entered this place, a raven cawed. She opened her eyes on a shimmering, electric blue field, perhaps sky, but it was around and beneath her and solid where she lay on it. The raven flew over her, its black wings motionless, riding a swift current of air, then it returned to a light on a spruce branch she hadn't noticed before. Perhaps the Indian beliefs of her youth prompted a hallucination. The bird spoke in the voice of a young girl. "I am your helper. Your father sent me. Stay there and rest." Then the vision was gone, and Maggie slept.

Gradually, she was covered by the heavily falling snow that built up above her perch and then slid softly down by the force of its own weight. She was buried like the arctic grouse which takes refuge from blizzards and cold by folding its wings high above snow-covered berry bushes and plummeting into them to gain the insulating warmth of the rapidly growing blanket of snow.

Thunder's search for Maggie was as fruitless as Dolf's. No one could think of anything to say to alleviate Dolf's grief. The Hummingbird stood eloquently before him, tears blinding her; then she hugged him. "I so sad," she mumbled brokenly. Later, she brought him a plate of food and a steaming cup of coffee. To himself he said, "I so sad, too." He knew he would be lonely the rest of his life. He drank a little coffee. He gave the food to Jim Too, who ate it, then lay, head on his paws, doleful eyes on Dolf's face, aware of Dolf's mood if not necessarily of the circumstances that had caused it.

Dolf lay awake in his robes, conscious of being alone. Jim Too occasionally burrowed beneath the outer tarp, sometimes sighing, then going out into the blizzard and later returning. Dolf knew he was searching for what had been a great part of his existence, too. But Maggie had been the whole warm glow by which Dolf had lived. He remembered how she'd felt in his arms, her gentle warm breath on his cheek or neck, sighing contentedly in the knowledge that she was secure and loved.

Toward light he pushed back his covering. Stars were visible. A faint hint of the rippling borealis flashed once or twice, then was banished by the sun, which neared the horizon, casting its rosy blush before it. He stared at the sky, watching it lighten. A sudden howl startled him. Wolves, he thought—for an instant. But the next howl identified itself as Jim Too's distinctive hound bugle. His first thought was,

Maggie! Maybe he's found her. he leaped out of his robes and headed toward the dog, his black silhouette visible near where Maggie had vanished. Elation overwhelmed him. Faithful old Jim Too might have found Maggie. Perhaps she was still alive. Then the probable truth superseded that notion. "My God," he told himself. "She'd be frozen by now even if she had been alive and we'd missed her."

He ploughed through drifts toward the dog who was crouched at the brink of the cliff, alternately looking down and at him. Dolf halted at the edge. On a ledge some ten feet below, something was stirring. Soon a snow-covered apparition rose from the center of a bush and looked up at them.

"Dolf!" Maggie cried, extending her arms and almost losing her balance. "Dolf! It's me! I'm alive!" She tried to clamber up the sheer rock above her, with only the notion of reaching him in her mind.

"Stay there!" he yelled. Then he disappeared, just as he had in her dream. Am I dead? she wondered. Is this how it's going to be?

She knew she wasn't dead when he reappeared and tossed the rope form where he'd left it coiled, intending to search for her again this day. He shinnied quickly down to her and embraced her fiercely. She had never before seen tears in his eyes, but they were there now.

"I thought you were dead," he said in a hoarse voice. "My God, I thought you were dead. I love you so much, Maggie."

Beyond Miles the river provided a broad highway. Dolf relentlessly drove them on, battling numbing cold, blizzards, short rations, and constant fatigue. Maggie doggedly plowed along behind him day after day, both sustained and driven by the constant knowledge that even minutes could mean the margin between life and death for their foster daughter. She dreamed of Little Maggie every night, seeing the jolly, chubby, little face, her black eyes bright as shiny marbles, sparkling with mischief and the joy of living. The mite would run toward her, reaching out her arms to be scooped up and hugged as she had so often been. Margaret would pick her up, warm, soft and yielding, feeling the strong little arms hugging her neck tightly. Then, suddenly, the child would become cold and stiff in her arms. She would awake in paralyzed denial of what she realized must have happened. Once she cried aloud from her dream, "No! No! No!" Dolf woke her up with a comforting embrace.

"You were dreaming," he said. "What was it?"

She didn't tell him. Didn't have to.

At least they were never again totally halted by blizzards. The river was fringed by timber or cliffs that guided them if they veered from that course.

Days and nights became a blur in Maggie's consciousness until finally they reached Fort Reliance. Compared to what they'd traversed, it now seemed only a few miles—though it was almost a hundred.

Jack McQuesten, who ran the trading post for the A.C. Company, urged them to rest for at least a day. "You folks are wore to a nub," he stated the obvious. "Might git thar jist as quick if yuh rest up a day."

Dolf shook his head. "Cain't rest now, Jack." He looked at Maggie. "Why don't you stay?"

Her expression alone answered, but she said, "I know how to give vaccinations. None of the rest of you do."

They left some of their lemon extract at the fort before pulling out after only an hour's breather. Jack had provided them with several fresh dogs. Heavy new snow was pouring down again from a lowering sky, growing heavier every minute, eventually retarding their progress to a mere snail's pace. Margaret found herself biting her lip. What bothered her most, she realized, could be completely irrational. She had experienced the truth of one dream, and now was haunted by the possibility that another would be fulfilled. But the question was—which scene would be played out in the end? Or would both occur in sequence; their finding Little Maggie alive only to lose her because she had not been vaccinated in time—or from some other reason entirely? At least Margaret somehow felt certain that Little Maggie was still alive, though she couldn't have said why she felt this way.

Their last camp was the shortest of all. Dolf, driven by the same terrible fears as Maggie, roused the camp after only four hours rest. A foot or so of added snow had fallen, blanketing the camp so that they had to dig and shake their way out. They did this hastily, downed some hot tea and biscuits, then hitched the dogs and mushed out. A weak sun rose, partly visible through thinning clouds, which drifted apart to reveal patches of radiant blue sky. The shoreline was now distinct, making it a simple matter to identify the mouth of the Sky Pilot fork. They veered into its icy channel, shouting encouragement to the dogs. They were less than two miles form St. John. Maggie felt her fatigue leaving her, buoyed by relief and hope as well as the adrenalin that drives a runner across the finish line still feeling fresh. Smoke from many wood fires, rising in pillars on the still air, was visible beyond the sloping margin of willow and spruce. This friendly odor of civilization also keyed her up.

Dolf led the way directly to Old John's trading post, pulling up abreast the full-length porch. Side by side, he and Maggie rapidly mounted the steps. She stumbled, feeling faint, and he steadied her.

Someone opened the door a foot—but no further. Dolf and Margaret paused, unaware that someone had seen them coming and that Elsie Hedley had put Little Maggie up to a special reception for them.

An elfin, little head poked around the door, grinning. "Mommy! Daddy!" she cried, rushing out to them. Maggie swept her up first, Dolf embracing both of them in a huge hug. Tears were streaming down Maggie's cheeks. She didn't miss the mistiness in Dolf's eyes either, even though he was grinning. She loved him more than she ever had.

"Thank God," she whispered. "Thank God."

John and Elsie pulled everyone inside, the women taking Little Maggie to the kitchen to vaccinate her. Old John uncorked a supply of what the men needed most just then. Dolf made an exception to his usual "just one."

Sprawled in one of John's big moosehide thong chairs, his outer garments tossed on the floor, a lit cigar in his mouth, he let out a huge sigh.

"Thank Christ, John," he said.

"Fer the seegar and booze?"

"Them too."

Margaret and Elsie had had a small tussle with Little Maggie, who tearfully accepted her medicine with her lower lip sticking out. Assurances of "it's good for you" hadn't cut much ice with her. It hurt.

Now the savory odors of food overcame the trading post's pungent odor of furs, blankets, spices, preservatives, tobacco, coal oil, as well as the smokiness characteristic of cabins in the north.

Dolf told John, "I know Maggie half-died the whole way thinkin' you were all down with smallpox or scurvy. Anybody here have it?"

"Nope," John assured him. "We was jist lucky on the smallpox, but you know I always keep a leetle stash of private dry fruit and spuds and the like." He winked. "We weren't hurtin' yet, but you got here jist in time. Some o' the boys out in the diggin's 'll be damn glad to get some of that lemon. Had some smallpox out there too, but only a few cases. Plenty of the Injuns died from it though, like they always do—the poor buggers."

One day as Maggie was busy in her improvised clinic at Old John's trading post, Dolf slipped in and raised the window without saying a word. "Listen," he said.

The eaves were dripping. Spring was near. Soon the ice would go out, and Little Henry would be coming in on the first river steamer.

CHAPTER 20

THE *Idaho* docked at Juneau on May 30, 1889 for a two-day stop before continuing on to St. Michael. This was its first trip to the Yukon that year. On board were Dolf's best friend Doc Hennessey, Dolf's grandmother Mum, and his son, Henry.

Juneau's streets were decked with flags and patriotic bunting for the third of four Memorial Day celebrations. They had already celebrated two Confederate memorials that year—one on April 26, the next on May 10—and would celebrate the third on June 3. The frontier was a democratic place! Juneau's leading Democrat was a strong Republican—Blunderbuss Newgast. He allowed that the Rebs had as much right to celebrate as anyone, parlticularly when the drinks were on them. (Everyone was drunk or on the way—except Stan King.) To Stan's sour remark that the Rebs' celebrations were probably treasonable, Newgast had retorted, "Hell, Stan, we're fightin' 'em best two outa three. It ain't even been settled yet." Verbally, at least, that was true, and no one had even been killed yet. Of course it was only 11 A.M. The periodic eruption of gunfire had only been target practice at the sun, which showed no evidence of damage.

The *Idaho* had a temporary captain due to Magruder's suspicion that Juneau might welcome his return too warmly. Cap had hand-picked Tom Tom Tidball as just the right replacement, coaxing him into a swap for the Hawaiian run. Rumor had it that Cap was in Honolulu teaching Princess Liliuokalani to cuss in English and to drink Scotch. No one doubted it.

Tom Tom was the acknowledged bare-knuckle champion

of the West Coast merchant fleet. It wasn't surprising. He stood six foot seven and weighed three hundred and ten pounds.

A typical story was of the fabled bout in which he'd vanquished a belligerent Irish ship's captain of equal weight. Tom Tom's retort to the complaint that he had the reach on his opponent was vintage Tom Tom. "Hell," he'd said. "We're about the same height. He's five-five and I'm only five-nineteen." The Irishman had bawled, "Come down here where I can reach yer ugly mug." Instead, Tom Tom had stood him on a box, given him six free swings which he adroitly dodged, then tossed him off the wharf where the fray had taken place.

The Morgette party was receiving the royal treatment from Tom Tom due to a letter sent by Dolf to the *Idaho's* principal owner, Ira Baker, by way of Billy Moore just before Dolf had left for White Pass, The substance of it read:

December 4, 1888

Dear Ira,

We are leaving for St. John through the interior to carry in smallpox vaccine and lemon juice to fight scurvy. They're having a hell of a bout of both in there.

He then related how Gabriel Dufan had carried that news to the outside, adding the details of recent happenings in Juneau that had at least temporarily rendered him and Maggie fugitive. He'd been sure Cap Magruder would send Ira similar details. He then continued:

I suspect it would be a good idea to try to get Old John appointed a U.S. Commissioner next year. It wouldn't hurt if I could get an appointment again as U.S. Deputy Marshal. Maybe Alby Gould can help. (He was referring to their mutual friend, Senator Alby

Gould, who'd obtained him a similar commission in '86.)

Finally he'd written:

> My grandmother is escorting our son Henry up to St.
> John on the first trip the *Idaho* makes in the spring. An
> old friend, and family doctor, Doc Hennessey, will be
> with them. I suspect Cap Magruder may not be on that
> run. (This was tongue-in-cheek since he knew damn
> well he wouldn't and that Ira knew why.) So would you
> ask the new captain to kind of look out for them for my
> sake.
>
> Sincerely,
Dolf

The latter request had assured them royal treatment,
though Mum and Tom Tom would have sniffed one another out as kindred spirits by some psychological chemistry
even without Dolf's request. As it was, Tom Tom had met
her and the others at the gangplank. He'd eyed the long
parcel carried by Mum, suspecting its contents. After intro-
ductions, Tom Tom's first words were, "I'll carry that pack-
age for you, if you'd like." Mum was also carrying young
Henry.

"Not on yer tintype," she snapped.

"What the heck's in it?" Tom Tom asked.

"M' double-barrel shotgun. I don't miss much with it,
either."

"Why use two barrels, then?" he asked.

"In case one don't shoot fer enough."

That was the beginning of a pleasant voyage—Mum's
first—at which she enjoyed a seat at the captain's table. As
they warped in at Juneau, Mum and Henry were watching
from the bridge next to Tom Tom.

"Sounds like the Fourth of July," Mum observed.

"Wait'll tonight. It gets better." This wasn't Tom Tom's first holiday in the Alaskan port. "If yer plannin' to go sightseeing, better wait'll I can go along."

Mum gave him a laden look which he expected and pretended not to notice. It plainly said, "Humph." What she said was, "We never lost nuthin' there. If we go I kin take care o' myself, 'n the kid too. M' hometown'd make this look like Sunday School." That was true.

Doc, however, decided to mosey uptown. The first establishment that coaxed him in with its wares was the Skookum. In less then half an hour he was in on a high stakes poker game. It was the way he'd spent every free evening for at least his past ten years, and he wasn't a pauper yet. A little past 2 A.M., with all the money around in front of him and no fresh meat in sight, he observed, "I guess I'll buy the drinks and head home."

Three of the shorn, now house fixtures, were Shiv Filetti, Schoolboy Mumma, and Lobo Lafferty. Since she had plans for them, Nilda kept them at least nominally on her payroll—i.e., whenever their luck ran out at the games downstairs. It didn't happen very often, and never to the extent that it had at Doc's hands.

"Where's home?" Shiv asked. "I don't believe I've seen you around."

"I'm brand-new," Doc said, eying him for hostile intentions. Doc had seen his type before. The other two didn't escape accurate cataloging in Doc's mind, either. They all spelled bad news.

"You didn't answer the man's question," Logo put in, sounding ominous.

Doc looked him in the eye, appearing less amiable than he had. "You fellows figurin' on a trip out back with me?"

Schoolboy chimed in. "Nothing that crude." He laughed. "The boss'd like to see you upstairs."

"Tell him to come the hell down if he'd like to see me," Doc said, remaining seated with his back to the wall. He continued to stack his bills and coins. He was outwardly nonchalant, but watched covertly for any hostile move.

"It's a 'she,'" Schoolboy said.

"You wouldn't want to disappoint a lady, would you?" Lobo asked, moving his hand slowly toward his belt.

None of them were sure where the .41 Colt Lightning in Doc's hand came from. "Send her down," he said. "I'll be here for about another five minutes." The .41 disappeared as smoothly as it had appeared. Doc looked them over coldly and sipped his whiskey.

Shiv left and returned a short while later with Nilda in trail. She took a seat at the table, treating Doc to her blinding smile and batting blue eyes. Women weren't Doc's weakness.

He eyed her, poker-faced. "Spit it out, sister," he said.

She hadn't expected that, but managed to keep the blinding smile glued to her face. "How'd you like a job?"

Doc was surprised, but very little ever shocked him. Dolf had also dropped him a note before leaving Billy Moore's. He was aware of the winter's events—especially about what had happened to Goldie, Lobo's attempt to kill Dolf, and the new setup at the Skookum. Principally, Dolf had wanted to make sure that no one tried to get at him and Maggie through little Henry. For that reason, Doc had persuaded Mum to travel under the name Hennessey. It had taken some tall talking. Now Nilda's offer struck Doc as a God-given chance to find out what some of Dolf's enemies might be up to, particularly Lobo. He had hoped Lobo would continue his play with the six-shooter. He'd have loved to relieve Dolf of that threat.

"What's the deal?" he asked Nilda.

"You make the pasteboards talk, I'm told. I got a job for you at the place I'm gonna open up on the Yukon."

"Dealin?" Doc asked.

"That—and some other things. If you're interested, drop around tomorrow about four and I'll fill you in. You'll have to make up your mind before day after tomorrow, because we're leaving on the *Idaho* to go up there."

Doc read that as meaning that she wanted some more time to talk it over with the rest of her crew before deciding how much—if anything—she wanted to tell him.

The first "talking over" took place right after Doc left—in the clubroom, as Nilda didn't want to risk having Hubie overhear any of it. He was, by then, living in her apartment, much to the disgust of Shiv Filetti. However, he knew a good thing and wasn't pushing his luck. He was seeing her regularly in one of the other rooms.

"Well," Nilda started the conversation, "you boys all seem to have had a bad night." She laughed. "We all have our off days," she added.

" 'Off day,' hell," Shiv said. "Jesus Christ himself couldn't take money off that bastard at poker. He knows all the tricks. He's so good I couldn't even see him when I knew damn well he was stackin' the deck." It was a tribute to the nimble hands that had also made Doc the best gunshot surgeon in the country.

"Me neither," Schoolboy confessed. "And I thought I was good. Funny I never heard of him."

Actually, they had, but they were misled by thinking of him only as a gambler. Besides, he hadn't been in the news for ten years.

"Maybe from back East," Lobo guessed.

Shiv said, "Not likely, the way he unlimbered that cannon. Maybe New Orleans or Texas."

Nilda interrupted. "Anyhow, we need him, I think. I know none of you boys want to stay up North permanently. If he's that good and shows up here he could be on the dodge—most likely is. That way he'll stick. I aim to keep the place up there open even after we scoop the cleanup. No one'll suspect me. You boys'll probably have to cut and run."

That brought a general murmur of approval. Nilda continued, "Schoolboy, you buddy up to him and see what you can learn about him. You, too, Lobo."

Lobo shook his head. "That might not be too easy after that gun business." Then he paused, looking thoughtful. "On the other hand, if I apologize to him real nice, that could give me an in." Lobo had his shrewd side.

Schoolboy, one of the best cons in the business, agreed. He said, "A shrewd move. There's no friend like an old enemy."

"Besides," Lobo said. "I'd really like to find out who he is. I'm bettin' 'Hennessey' ain't his real name."

"How much do we tell him about heisting the cleanup?" Schoolboy asked.

Nilda didn't hesitate. "Not a damn word. I want him to stick, not blow."

The next afternoon at 4 P.M. Doc was employed by Mrs. Carlson's little girl, Nilda. The deal was cut in her apartment. Afterward, she invited Doc to dinner. To her surprise, he accepted. She didn't realize he was on a fishing trip.

When he wished, Doc could have charmed alligators from a swamp onto a dance floor and, moreover, gotten Southern belles to dance with them. He charmed Nilda and Hubie at dinner, not realizing the possible consequences. Nilda had a fatal weakness for educated gentlemen. Doc wasn't entirely impervious to the ladies, either. He thought they were like Yosemite—great scenic attractions to visit occasionally, but too much bother to own and too expensive to keep. Therefore, the women he'd known were mostly of Nilda's persuasion. He had his suspicions as to where the evening was leading when she disposed of Hubie on an errand after dinner.

After he had gone she came straight to the point. "Shall we?" she asked.

Doc grinned. "Why not?" He'd inventoried Nilda's visible assets as soon as he'd laid eyes on her.

She led the way down the hall to her enticement chamber. Before long she was discovering that her new card mechanic knew more about female anatomy than anyone she'd ever known.

"My!" she gasped. "I just never knew."

"I'm not surprised," Doc said. He wasn't either.

She almost decided on the spur of the moment to confide her whole plan to him. But not quite. A poor girl learns not to trust anyone. If her plan went well, Hubie would be her ace in the hole. She'd learned that the main cleanup would go out of St. John in Baker and Hedley's safe. If she could work guileless Hubie into gaining Old John's confidence and becoming his accountant, the safe could go out empty. Of course, there was Rudy Dwan to work the same angle, but she wasn't as sure of him.

The big problem would be getting the stuff out of the safe and hidden away the night before shipment—under the midnight sun at that. She'd already solved that problem in her mind. There were a number of ways. Which one she picked would depend on circumstances. She'd learn more after she reached St. John. Rudy Dwan would be her pigeon. She knew he had a weakness for women—especially for her. Best of all was the fact that the others in her employ would take the rap. They'd run for it with an empty safe. If they weren't caught, no one would ever know but them. And they weren't apt to come back and complain. At least she hoped they wouldn't.

She smiled now, partly because these days that plan was constantly in her mind, but more because Doc had done something she particularly liked.

He noticed, but didn't ask the normal question. She'd have a whole boat trip to spill her thoughts to him, and he'd discovered you learn more by pretending you don't want to know.

CHAPTER 21

THE *Idaho* weighed anchor out of Juneau and headed north, carrying a starkly contrasting cast of characters. There was the crew, rowdy enough for anyone: Tom Tom on the bridge seconded by Alphabet Tullywine, Hop Sing in the galley to please or poison palates as he felt the occasion demanded, and Luna Montiero on hand in case someone needed service with a Winchester or belaying pin. Dolf's family and friends, respectable and interested in remaining as anonymous as possible, were balanced by Nilda and Company: the girls attracting a lot of attention from miners headed back north for the summer, the foremost among them in eye appeal being Lizzie LaBelle. The three goons—Shive, Schoolboy, and Lobo—were on board, strictly on their good behavior.

Doc, who'd been well-known for a season in the North, had a little problem, but he carefully watched the gangplank until everyone had boarded. He saw no one he recognized. The North was a place with a definitely shifting population. Little Henry posed a problem, as professional gamblers don't usually travel with nephews, so Doc made up to him openly their first day on board to assure that no one would be suspicious when the kid called him "Uncle Johnny." He was so successful in his act that Nilda told him, "You sure have a way with kids." Then added, "And women." They were in Doc's cabin when she said it.

They crossed to St. Michael on an unusually calm sea. By then Lobo thought he had recruited Doc to help them dispose of Dolf. He didn't disclose their motive, letting it appear to be strictly revenge. Lobo told Doc, "You might be faster'n him with a Colt. Might be able to take him head on."

"Why do it that way?" Doc asked. "No need to take chances."

"We don't aim to," Lobo assured him. "I was just callin' 'em like I see 'em. I'd have got him the safe way before now if someone hadn't butted in at the last minute. Maybe you'd like to keep him busy in front this time while I plant a lead pill right about where his suspenders cross?"

"Why not?" Doc said.

At St. Michael Nilda surreptitiously checked on the condition of the late Goldie's racing steamboat. It was completed and had been named the *Greyhound*. She told the tough gang Goldie had installed to build and run it (which was headed by an old Mississippi and Missouri river man, Hank Mountain), that they'd be working for her now. Mountain said, "Your money is as good as his, ain't that right, boys?" None groused, though most men in those days were a trifle squeamish about working for women. Mountain was a seasoned product who'd seen a lot of rough stuff and taken plenty of chances. Although Nilda didn't know, it, he was ready to take on plenty more long ones—for he wanted a stake to retire on somewhere.

Mountain had shrewdly let out the word that the *Greyhound* was his. To forestall suspicions about its speedy design, he had stated his intention, of cornering the mail business on the Yukon—now that the country was beginning to fill up and it was worthwhile. What he hadn't let on was that he'd been slowly filling the ship's secret coal bunkers with coal all winter, a gunny sack at a time. This would give him long odds in a chase on the Yukon, where the other boats would have to stop for wood.

Mountain's crew wasn't fully aware of what their mission would be—except that it might involve a fight. Both Goldie and Mountain had agreed to the need for absolute secrecy. The *Greyhound's* agenda was to follow the *Ira Baker*, on which the *Idaho's* passengers would be going upriver, find a secluded tributary in which to anchor, then contact Nilda for further orders at St. John.

After Nilda had left, Mountain drew aside his mate, Charlie Harris, and said, "Just between us I don't see any reason not to cut out that gal if we get the chance. What say?"

Harris shrugged and grinned. "You took the words right out of my mouth. I never hankered after workin' fer no skirt anyhow."

At St. Michael Doc had spotted a few old-timers who would recognize him, so he kept to his cabin on the upriver trip. Nilda let it out that he had the flu and that she was taking care of him. The latter was eminently true. Doc emerged on deck just before they were ready to debark at St. John. He saw Lobo in the crowd and on impulse grabbed him by the arm. He said, "If this Morgette is up here like you think, and if he's the kind of hairpin you say he is, he'll be lookin' over whoever comes in—especially on the first boat."

In fact, Doc had already spotted Dolf and Margaret in the crowd. He'd known they'd be here, waiting anxiously for Henry and Mum to debark. Lobo said, "I'd better lay low, but that's Morgette out there, all right—with the gal holdin' on his arm—the tall guy in the big black hat. Prob'ly got two six-shooters on him."

Doc eyed Lobo with exaggerated suspicion written on his face. He almost sneered. "You scared o' him? C'mon. I'll back yuh if he makes a play. My guess is he won't. Not with womenfolks around. You don't want the word to get out that yer yellow, do you?"

Lobo paled perceptively. He bought Doc's conclusion and saw that he had more to lose by hanging back than making a bold front of it.

He followed Doc down the gangplank—nervous, but not nearly as nervous as Doc had it in mind for him to be. Dolf spotted Doc and Lobo, walking ahead of Mum and little Henry. He and Maggie moved rapdily forward, but then Dolf caught Doc's warning look and a big wink. "Wait a minute, Maggie," he said, "Doc's got something up his sleeve." She could see that for herself, though the sight of Lobo aroused her blood. She'd have finished the job on him with a knife if she'd had one and no one was around—part of her was pure Indian and always would be. Dolf figured Doc had the situation under control and waited for his cue. It wasn't long in coming. Doc leaped to one side, exposing Lobo, then yelled, "Okay Morgette. Me and Lobo are here to settle yore hash. Go fer yer guns!"

Lobo almost yelped, "No! I ain't heeled! Are you nuts, Doc?" He quickly back-pedalled away, tripping on the stringer plank at the edge of the dock and disappearing downward where a splash announced his arrival in the Sky Pilot some fifteen feet below. Doc had jerked his pistol and fired a couple of shots in the air before Lobo landed. People were flying for cover in all directions. Then Doc peered over the edge, having trouble keeping a straight face—Lobo was floundering around trying to stay afloat, his boots rapidly filling with water. "Go for the ladder," Doc directed him, pointing it out. Lobo made it, sputtering and gasping. "I got him," Doc yelled down by way of encouragement. Finally Lobo made it up the ladder, a grin about to capture his face. It never quite formed. His first sight was of Dolf and Doc, arm in arm. He almost fell back into the Sky Pilot again. Doc snorted. "I fergot to tell you, Lobo. Me and Dolf are old friends."

Lobo's expression was hard to catalog; obviously his mind was working rapidly. Finally he called up what had been bothering him—a recollection of the decade-old range war that had made the national newspapers: *"Dolf Morgette"* and *"Doc Hennessey"* had been featured frequently side by side in the captions. "My gawd," Lobo gasped. "I shoulda figured— yer *Doc* Hennessey."

"Yeah," Doc said. "I'm *Doc* Hennessey. And if I was you I'd get back on the *Ira Baker* and stay there, and be on it when it pulls out."

That was how Skookum Doc finally came home to St. John. His entrances were seldom routine. Only after his little act did the family reunion of Morgettes take place. Doc joined them as they walked up to the new Morgette cabin, which he hadn't yet seen. He still had his own cabin waiting for him, built in '86.

Lobo had gone back up the gangplank as Doc suggested, passing Schoolboy on the way. "C'mon back up to the cabin," Lobo said. "I gotta talk to you."

Schoolboy joined him after loitering long enough to be sure Dolf and Doc were gone.

"What's up?" Schoolboy asked. He'd witnessed Lobo's funny confrontation and had a pretty good idea.

Lobo said, "I'm gonna hafta disappear as far as Morgette and Hennessey know. I figure to join Mountain on the *Greyhound,* wherever the hell it is."

"Waddaya want me to do?" Schoolboy asked.

"I ain't sure," Lobo said. "This tub is goin' on up to Fort Reliance, so I'll drop up there on it and then get word to yuh. I aim to beef Morgette or die tryin'. That goes double for that bastard Hennessey."

Schoolboy figured that Lobo's chances of dyin' tryin' looked pretty fair, but he knew better than to argue with him. He shrugged. Maybe Lobo would get one or the other. He'd have liked to have Morgette out of the way when it came down to heisting the spring cleanup—even though he was sided by a tough crew like Mountain's.

"What should I tell Nilda?" Schoolboy asked.

"I dunno," Lobo said. "I guess she saw what happened. Tell her I'll be on the *Greyhound*, if I can find it. Maybe it'll be up at Fort Reliance. In any case, I'll be back before you pull the job."

Schoolboy debated mentioning something that had been

on his mind for quite awhile. He decided to spill it. "Did you ever wonder where we stand in this deal the way things have shaped up now?" he asked.

"Waddaya mean?" Lobo looked puzzled.

"I mean we stand to maybe get cut out with Shiv and Nilda bein' just like that." He noted the light of interest kindling in Lobo's eyes and went on. "In fact, what's to keep Mountain and that crew of his from pullin' out on all of us?"

"You an' me're supposed to be on the *Greyhound* to see they don't".

"Strikes me as a pretty good way fer us to git killed, in case they aim to. There's a lot more o' them than us." Schoolboy looked thoughtful. "I think you 'n me better have a leetle confab with this guy Hank Mountain."

Lobo asked, "What the hell do we tell him?"

"I ain't sure yet. But we got time to think about that. You find the *Greyhound* and size up Mountain. Then slip in here and see me, or send somebody in and I'll come out and meet you in the brush."

Lobo nodded. "Slippin' in suits me fine. I'll drygulch them two if I get a chance."

"Don't forget it don't get dark around here this time of year."

"I ain't forgot. I can get 'em at four or five hundred yards from out in the brush."

"Pretty chancy, I'd say."

Lobo flushed. "You ain't seen me shoot."

"I've heard, but five hundred yards is still a long ways."

"I'll get 'em at five feet if I can slip that close."

"Suit yourself," Schoolboy said, heading for the door. "And be sure to get in touch as soon as you can."

Beyond a doubt, the key actor in the next few weeks should have been Nilda. She figured she held all the high cards, all the key knowledge. Her money would ensure that she could pull all the strings she had to to make the actors perform. One possible fly in the ointment was that Nilda was in love by the time she reached St. John. The lucky target of her burning passion was Doc Hennessey. Even after she found out his true identity, it made no difference. She had nothing against Dolf, merely seeing him as a possible obstacle to her plans. If it all worked out as she had in mind, there was no reason to put him out of the way.

Nilda's being in love with Doc was not the least of the reasons that Hubie had fallen out of love with Nilda. His heart had been battered all winter, long before Doc had entered the picture. He knew that Nilda was frequently down the hall in some room or other with Shiv. Doc was simply the last straw. Hubie wasn't blind, or dumb, and, despite his deceptive appearance he was no doormat.

En route to St. John, Hubie had seen a lot of Lizzie La-Belle. Nilda had been too busy to even notice, or to care if she did. She was sure Hubie would remain under her thumb anyway. Hubie and Lizzie frequently could be seen holding hands, standing at the rail of the *Idaho* and later the *Ira Baker*, quietly watching the water or the scenery on shore slip past.

There was a lot of the right stuff in Hubie. Nilda had underestimated him. Dolf had not. Neither had Lizzie.

On the Yukon one evening, near the Ramparts, Lizzie released a mammoth sigh, as though something were weighing heavily on her mind.

"What's the matter, honey?" Hubie asked.

She looked pensively at the hills which appeared to be slowly receding downstream, then at the water, finally at Hubie. "Girls like me ain't supposed to fall in love," she confessed.

"Why not?" he asked. "You're just as good as anybody else." But her words had driven a knife into his ribs. He suspected she was about to confide in him like a big brother and say whom she was in love with. He'd had a lot of practice taking his lumps from the opposite sex—since before first grade right on up through his recent experience with Nilda. Now he was in love with Lizzie, but would never have told her so for fear she'd laugh. He was grateful he'd had her a little while, and that she'd done the nice things she'd done without making him pay.

She directed the conversation away from love, sensing it had troubled him but misjudging his reason. She went on, "I always just wanted a farm and a family like Ma. Lots of farm women hated it, but she never did. I wouldn't either." She sighed again.

Hubie waited for her to continue if she felt like it. She looked directly into his eyes. "You know my real name back in Nebraska is Beckie Brewster?"

He dumbly wondered why, if it were Beckie Brewster in Nebraska, it might not be the same here. He heard her say, "I got a letter from Ma before we left Juneau. She thinks I'm a nurse. Said her and Pa was gettin' too old to run the place and wished I was married so we could come back and run it." She let out a short laugh, but there was no joy in it. "Then she said she knew I had a good job and would never do that." A tear formed in her eye, then another. They slowly rolled down the side of her nose. Suddenly she rushed into Hubie's arms. "I'd love to do that," she snuffled, broken-voiced.

He held her tenderly. "Who's the skunk that won't marry you?" he growled. "I'd do it in a minute."

She tensed in his arms. He could feel the sudden stiffness in her as she pushed away. He thought he'd offended her. "I'm sorry," he said quickly.

"For what?" she asked.

"Because I know I'm fat and homely and dumb," he said. "I never should have sounded like I thought a good looker like you would marry me. I didn't mean to insult you—I just meant any man oughta be glad to marry you, was all. I never did know what to say to women," he concluded dolefully.

She laughed, tears still in her eyes. She said, "You big lovable ox, you just said the nicest thing any man could say. I'm in love with *you*."

That stunned him; it was the last thing he'd expected to hear. "Why?" he blurted.

She shook her head. "I don't know. I don't care. I just am."

Shortly they disappeared into his and Nilda's cabin. He knew Nilda wasn't using it any more—not even to wash her face.

Nilda was happy to discover that Old John Hedley had a nice, big, empty basement under the trading post that he'd rent her to store her beer till she got set up at the Skookum Too. She could have rented it strictly on a business basis, but that didn't satisfy her ego. She tossed into the bargain a little eye-batting and wiggling of what she wiggled best—which was a bunch. Old John took in the performance with relish. He said, "Jist any leetle favor I k'n do fer you, ma'am, 'll be my pleasure." Happily for him (and Nilda) Elsie wasn't there. She was likely to have kicked Old John and scalped Nilda.

Nilda recognized John's offer as the opening she was looking for. "For one thing," she told him hesitantly, "would it be asking too much to have the key so my men can get in day or night?"

"Hell no, that makes sense," John said. "I was figgerin' you'd want it. Nothin' down there now except dust. I think there may be a squirrel livin' there, but he won't drink up yer beer." He guffawed.

Nilda had already bought another building to house the Skookum Too. It was the big two-story cabin that had formerly been the now-defunct Brown and Shadley trading post—Old John's former competitors.

She and John shook on their deal. Old John allowed, "This camp needed a regular joint." He was wondering if Nilda helped out the girls when things got going full blast. "I'm gettin' too dern old to bust up fights at my place, and so far that's the only likker joint in camp."

Nilda was temporarily boarding with Doc—an arrangement that pleased them both. Dolf kidded Doc mildly about it. "That's some heifer you got," was about the extent of it, though. Margaret was graciously silent about it, much to Doc's relief. As Nilda left Old John's to return there, she congratulated herself on having gotten over one hurdle in her plan. She now knew she could probably heist the spring cleanup without rough stuff. She didn't foresee any need for that when Hank Mountain pulled off the sham robbery and spirited the safe out of the country.

The thought had occurred to her, however, that Mountain, Lobo and Schoolboy—all of whom were scheduled to participate—might just run out on her. She laughed inwardly at that. None of them knew the safe would be empty. She had considered dispensing with their assisstance altogether, then thought better of it. If the safe got safely on the *Ira Baker* it was just possible that Old John could make a last minute check on it and find it empty. She wouldn't have time to get the loot out of his basement and safely away by then. The beer cases, of course, would provide the means of ferrying the gold from the basement to her own cache. She hadn't yet decided where that would be.

Right now her main consideration was getting Hubie a job with Old John so she would have someone to watch Rudy Dwan. Being cautious, she hadn't yet told Mountain everything that was expected of him, though he'd slipped into camp to report to her.

All in good time. She was learning the Machiavellian practice of not letting the right hand know what the left was doing.

She got ahold of Hubie (now that she knew it was feasible to carry out an inside job) and gave him his marching orders. She said, "I want you to ask Morgette to get you a job with Old John over at the store."

Hubie, not feeling overly happy with her, stubbornly asked, "Suppose I can't get the job?"

Nilda laughed. "You'll get it all right. Tell 'em you're tryin' to get away from the sinful business you found out your brother was running. That'll get 'em. They're all basically respectable. Their Christain upbringing'll get the best of 'em."

Hubie thought, Boy, if you only knew how bad I want to get away from the whole stinking business! But, unlike his brother, he sensed that Nilda could be dangerous. Besides, she still had at least two killers hanging around that he knew about. He was shrewd enough to figure out that Lobo wasn't too far away, either.

Hubie wondered why Dolf, now a deputy U.S. marshal, hadn't run Shiv and Schoolboy out of town too. He didn't understand the code that required Dolf to give them the first move. If he had, he'd have concluded that it was dumb.

Shiv and Schoolboy had had to find a cabin—as had Hubie—since the Skookum Too wasn't finished yet. Hubie would have liked to move Lizzie LaBelle in with him, taking her away from her life of sin, but they were both afraid of the possible consequences from Nilda. They'd talked it over and concluded they'd better wait. Since Nilda herself was now respectably in love and not taking an active hand in the business anymore, Lizzie had become Nilda's star attraction.

Hubie dutifully looked up Dolf and announced his mission.

"We'll just look into that," Dolf told him. "But first, how about joining us for dinner; we're about to sit down." Dinner there was the noon meal; supper was in the evening.

Hubie gratefully accepted. He hadn't had a decent meal since he'd arrived. He wasn't built for that. He'd been living on canned stuff from the trading post. After dinner he got up the nerve to mention something else that was bothering him. "Them two killers are still around," he said, meaning Shiv and Schoolboy.

Dolf merely nodded. He could guess what Hubie was thinking. He appreciated his concern and decided to put it to rest. He told him, "I know. But I reckon their fangs are pulled, now that Goldie's dead. He had a grudge against me. Nilda doesn't, as far as I know."

"I see," Hubie said. Only he didn't. He figured having such

people around was a risk on general principles. His conscience also bothered him over not telling Dolf why Nilda, also might want him out of the way. After dinner Dolf said, "let's you and me go over and see Old John about that job."

It didn't take much persuasion to get John Hedley to do a favor for Dolf. Besides, he really did need a bookkeeper. After he agreed to hire Hubie, Old John drew Dolf aside. "I don't give a damn if he *is* Goldie's brother. He looks dead square to me."

Hubie left with orders to report to work the next day. Dolf stayed to smoke and yarn with Old John in his office. Between them they were the U.S. Government in St. John, since Alby Gould had got Hedley an appointment as U.S. Commissioner. Hedley's office was, in a way, the federal building. They'd just gotten their cigars lit and were figuring out what improbable lies they could amuse one another with when a disturbance erupted outside. Rudy Dwan had obviously halted someone at the door, preventing an unceremonious entry into Old John's inner sanctum. The someone was loudly proclaiming, "I want to see the law, I don't care if it is busy. This won't wait."

Dolf looked at Old John. "Stan King," he said.

"Well," John replied, "we expected the son-of-a-bitch. Let's get it over with." He yelled to Dwan, "Send 'im in, Rudy."

Stan stalked in. "Where's the marshal?" he asked. He'd just come in on an A.C. Company boat, and someone had told him there was now a marshal—but obviously not who it was. Stan saw Dolf. "I got a warrant for you." Then, "Where's the marshal?" he asked Old John.

"I'm the marshal," Dolf told him. "You want me to serve that warrant on myself?" He was barely able to suppress a smile.

"Hell, no," Stan said. He looked around. "Where's the U.S. Commissioner? He can serve it."

Old John held out a hand. "I'm the Commissioner. Let me see the papers." King hesitated. "Gimme the goddam things!" Hedley commanded. "I'll turn you upside down an' take 'em if I have to."

King was aware that Old John might do just that. Reluctantly, he removed them from an inside pocket and handed them over.

Old John took his time scanning the documents. "Signed by that old tosspot Newgast," he finally said. "He ain't got any more say up here than a jack rabbit." He tore the papers in two and dropped them on the floor.

King's face turned red. "By God, I'm gonna have justice!" he shouted.

"Not likely," Old John said. "Unless we get a thunderstorm, and lightning strikes you." They all knew these were no thunderstorms that far north.

King gave Old John a killing look. He turned, saying over his shoulder, "I'll get up a miners' meetin'. Just wait."

"Grab him, Dolf," Old John ordered. Dolf didn't have to. Rudy Dwan had been listening outside and blocked the door. Seeing himself boxed in, King turned and bleated, "You can't do this."

Old John stabbed the air with his cigar to emphasize his remark. "The hell I can't. I'm convenin' court right here and now. You're tryin' to incite a riot. That's a federal offense." Old John didn't know whether it was or not. In fact, he didn't know whether a commissioner could convene a court, but he was sure none of the others did, either. As a matter of fact, the only things he was absolutely sure were against the law were robbery, rape, and murder. Nonetheless, it sounded good to him. To tone up the proceeding a trifle he said, "This here honorable court is in session." He turned to Dolf and asked, "Marshal, if I was to tell you to take this son-of-a-bitch out and hang him, what would you do?"

Dolf said, "Why, your honor, I'd take the son-of-a-bitch out and hang him."

King was speechless. He was perfectly convinced that they were capable of doing just that.

Old John said, "This court'll be lenient in yore case. I'm givin' you a blue ticket. Don't let the sun set on you around here." Then he remembered it wasn't apt to set until about late July. "I'm amendin' that order. Git on the next boat out and don't come back."

King sputtered. "I got a claim up here."

"Shoulda thought of that first. Marshal, escort this man to the boat."

On their way to the wharf Dolf did an unaccustomed thing. Before doing it, he considered that King—due to an irrational prejudice—was just as apt as not to try to get Maggie hanged solely because she was an Indian. He stopped King and said, "Look at me. I want to tell you something and you'd better listen good. If you ever come back here while I'm around, or try to bother my wife or me ever again, I'll kill you."

King was no fool. He knew Dolf. He turned pale.

"Is that clear?"

"It's clear," King said, badly shaken. He looked back once and stumbled as he did so, hurrying back up the gangplank that he'd rushed down just fifteen minutes before. He was still very pale.

While Dolf stood at the foot of the gangplank watching King, a heavy rifle slug whistled past his ear. He dove behind a pile of freight on the dock, jerking his .45 as he did so. He rolled on the planks then came up on his knee, cautiously scanning the area, then he dropped quickly back down. Only then did he feel the blood running down his neck. When he put his hand there, he found it covered with blood. He fished out his handkerchief and clapped it to the wound.

The sound of the shot had taken a couple of seconds to reach him, so he knew it was safe to bob up for a second to look around—unless there was a second ambusher nearer. He decided to risk it. He wasn't surprised to see that none of the few in sight had been disturbed by the sound of the shot. Shooting was too common around St. John. Sometimes moose even wandered into the village and were shot.

However, a roustabout on the steamer's deck had seen what had happened to Dolf. While heading for cover himself he yelled to Dolf, "Keep down. I'll take a good gander for you in a second."

Dolf turned and watched him disappear inside the deckhouse. Shortly, he peered around the edge of a door. "I don't see anybody," he yelled.

Then Stan King looked out briefly, took in the scene, and ducked. By then a few others sensed that something unusual had happened, and drifted to the scene. The dock was out of sight of St. John proper, the village wisely laid out above the flood plain ever since the spring flood a few years before. Dolf knew the shot had to have come from the hills back of town, at least a quarter of a mile away.

He thought, damn close shootin'. Lobo instantly came to mind. "I should have burned him down when Doc gave me the chance," he mumbled under his breath.

When he figured the coast was clear he started back to town, declining the company of a few who volunteered to go with him.

"Just a crease," he assured them. "It might not be safe too near me just now." He carefully watched the timber for any sign of movement as he went, though he would have bet that Lobo—or whoever the shooter had been—was long gone by then.

As Doc was stitching up the gash a little later, Dolf said, "Lobo, I bet. He'll be after you too, if I know him."

"Um," was all Doc volunteered. Then, "Hold still." When he was finished, he said, "Best we start packin' Winchesters. My guess is he won't get in six-shooter range."

CHAPTER 22

RUDY Dwan and Hubie hit if off from the first. The same was true with Hubie and Old John, although the latter accepted new friends very cautiously as a rule. He and his wife Elsie took to having Hubie to supper on a regular basis along with Rudy, who by then was practically a family member. When Hubie wasn't at supper with the Hedleys, he ate with the Morgettes. Henry and Little Maggie crawled onto Hubie's lap whenever he invited them, sensing he was the true article (as children often do, in some odd manner). Jim Too knew the same thing. Hubie felt truly wanted for the first time in his life. Naturally he was plagued by guilt, knowing what he'd been sent to do.

Moreover, he knew that Rudy Dwan was equally guilty. That really bothered him, since he felt Rudy was a truer brother to him than any of his own had been—especially Goldie. He wondered how Dwan, accepted as a member of Hedley's family, could scheme to rob him. It took awhile for Hubie to consider the possibility that Dwan might wonder the same about him. But in Hubie's opinion, Dwan was more the villainous type. He was a picture of a big, swarthy pirate, burly as a bear, with dark hair, handlebar mustache, and piercing black eyes.

Hubie may never have gotten up his nerve to quiz Dwan if he had not confided to him that he was in love.

"Who with?" Dwan asked.

"Lizzie LaBelle."

Dwan had the grace not to laugh.

"Hell, Kid," he said, "half the district's in love with her by now."

"But she's in love with me too."

"Wait a minute now," Dwan said. "I don't want no friend of mine hurt by no dance hall queen. What the hell do you mean?"

Hubie spilled the whole story.

"Well, I'll be go to hell," Dwan said. "You ain't joshin' me now?" But he knew Hubie wasn't capable of pulling his leg so convincingly.

"No," Hubie assured him. "It's true. Her name is really Beckie Brewster, and we aim to get hitched and go back to her folks' farm in Nebraska."

Dwan got a picture of it in his mind. He'd actually had the same general idea. Only he'd dreamed of a little ranch in Montana with a wife and a string of kids.

"Well, why the hell don't you drag her out of there and do it?"

"We ain't got the money. We're tryin' to save up. Besides, if I take her outa there, Nilda'll probably have me killed."

"The hell she will. Let's go see Morgette and Old John and have a weddin'."

"I can't yet, I'm still married."

"Cuts no ice up here," Dwan said.

"How about what we're supposed to do here?"

Dwan looked him over as if he were simple. He said, "You didn't really think I was gonna pull a job like that, or let a nice guy like you do it, did yuh?"

Hubie was stunned. "I guess I did," he said, sounding pretty lame.

"Let's just suppose we did what Nilda wants and someone like Old John opened that safe after we drained it. He might even do that if we loaded it up with buckshot bags like we're supposed to so it won't feel too light. Who'd end up holdin' the bag if he did that?"

The thought hadn't occurred to Hubie. It was obvious that he and Rudy would be the only logical suspects. They could hang for something like that. His breath shortened and he paled, his eyes growing big. "Us," he answered Rudy's question.

"Right," Rudy said. "Nilda must think we're damn dumb."

"I guess I was," Hubie confessed. "I never thought of that."

"I wouldn't pull no job like that on Old John, anyhow. He's just like family—so's his wife."

"What'll happen when Nilda finds out we didn't do it?"

Rudy shrugged. "Who cares? She don't give a damn what'd happen to us if we got caught."

They were unaware of Nilda's alternate plan in case they double-crossed her. The *Greyhound.*

"Now that that's settled, let's you and me go get yore gal outa that den of iniquity."

"They'll kill me," Hubie protested.

"Don't count on it," Dwan told him. "I'll have a leetle talk with Nilda, That oughta fix it up."

And it did. He threatened to squeal on her. "Besides, Hubie's a nice guy," he added.

Nilda had one word for that. "Shit!"

"Ain't we gonna squeal on Nilda, now that we've decided not to go through with it?" Hubie wondered.

"How'd we explain keepin' quiet this long? Beside, I'd rather have old blue eyes find out when she sends her boys to cart the dust outa Old John's basement and sees it ain't there."

Hubie shuddered. "She really will come after us then. Or send those killers, I mean."

"I doubt it. Besides, you'll be gone by then. So will I."

"Like I said, I ain't got any money to get outa here. Lizzie's got a little, but not enough."

"Don't worry. I got a wad. I'll pay our way out. You gave me the idea I wanta go back to Montana. I know a gal there that just might have me. A widdy with a raft of kids, so I reckon no one married her off yet."

"Suppose we can't pay you back for awhile?"

Dwan eyed him in a friendly fashion, putting a big hand on his arm and squeezing it. "Guys like me don't get a chance very often to feel like angels. Don't spoil it. I don't care if you never pay it back."

Lobo Lafferty found the *Greyhound* at Fort Reliance as he had hoped he would. He was uncertain about how he should approach Hank Mountain. Finally, he decided to tell him the whole story—except for his impromptu dip in the Sky Pilot.

Mountain looked him over critically, wondering if Nilda hadn't sent him to do some spying. He shrugged inwardly. He'd heard of Lafferty. Most men in the West had. Finally he said, "Dodgin' Morgette, eh? Cain't say as I blame yuh. I would."

Lobo wondered, in view of that, how dependable Mountain would be when the showdown came. It didn't occur to him that Mountain was wondering the same thing about him.

Lobo grimaced. "I'll git Morgette if I git another chance, don't worry about that."

Mountain nodded. "You'll get yer chance soon enough, form what I hear from our boss." He winked. "She's some looker. You had any o' that?"

It took Lobo by surprise. He guffawed. "Sure," he said. "She's in the business. Spent the whole winter down at her place. I'd be some kinda fool if I hadn't. Besides, she uses that cute tail o' hers to keep damn fools like us in line."

Mountain laughed. "I gotta run down to see her pretty soon. Reckon I oughta act like I'm gettin' outa line?"

Lobo was beginning to like Mountain. "Won't hurt to try," he said, "But she's taken a big shine to Morgette's sidekick Doc Hennessey. He might have somethin' to say about that. He's as pizen as Morgette."

Mountain shrugged "I hear she's got some other gals with her. What the hell." Then, "You suppose Doc Hennessey'll be with Morgette when they take the cleanup out?"

"I dunno. He might be. If he is, he ain't bulletproofed

either. If I git half a chance, I'll take both of 'em out before we pull the heist."

Mountain eyed him seriously. "I'll see you git that chance. I'm headin' back down there tomorra. Stay out of sight and I can slip you ashore somewhere before we git there. You might be seen by someone gittin' off at St. John. I aim to pull in and confab with my old sidekick Hedley. Him and me used to steamboat on the Missouri in the old days."

Lobo wondered what effect that might have on Nilda's plan. He liked the idea of maybe being able to set himself up somewhere for life after this deal. But it ruled out springing what he and Schoolboy had in mind—for the time being, at least.

Mountain stowed Lobo in his own cabin and put him ashore where the Yukon and Sky Pilot met. "You can work your way over to town and make your try on Morgette and Hennessey," Mountain said. "I'll pick you up here tomorrow night, most likely. Just wait. If anything goes wrong I'll send somebody down in a boat to let yuh know."

Lobo hiked over and sent a note to Schoolboy by a miner headed into town. It netted him a suspicious look, but the miner, like most in that country, was inclined to mind his own business. A ten dollar gold piece served to abate undue curiosity. Besides, a lot of good men were on the dodge from time to time. It was none of his business. Schoolboy got the note, bought the messenger a drink, and headed out to meet Lobo. The latter gave him his news about Mountain. "I don't see where it makes much difference in our plans. There's nuthin' we can do if Mountain tips our hand."

Schoolboy thought that over. "I don't think he will. I don't aim to tell Nilda that him and Old John might be thick, either. You just play along and see what turns up."

After Schoolboy left, Lobo concealed himself on the hill above St. John, scanning the place with a pair of field glasses he'd borrowed from Mountain. That was how he'd gotten his chance to take a shot at Dolf. He cursed under his breath when he realized he'd missed, but didn't try another shot for fear of giving away his position. Instead, he hightailed it back to his meeting place with Mountain. The latter showed up right on time. The first thing he said to Lobo when they were alone was, "You wouldn't know who took a pot shot at Morgette, would you?" He guffawed. "Nicked him in the neck. A couple of inches to one side and we wouldn't have to worry about him." Seeing Lobo's look he added, "Damn good shootin' at that range, though."

"Hard to figure the wind at that distance," was all Lobo said. "I'll git him when the time comes. When's that apt to be?"

"About three weeks the way I see it. We'll have time to make a run to St. Michael and back. If I hang around up here, somebody'll get suspicious sure as hell."

Lobo debated staying behind and trying for another shot at Dolf or Doc. But it didn't square with his and Schoolboy's plans. He decided to make the run down and maybe get a lot better acquainted with Mountain. His chance came in St. Michael after he and Mountain had sat in an all-night poker game. The latter had a few more drinks than he was used to. As they walked back to the *Greyhound* Mountain asked, "How well do you know that Nilda dame?"

Lobo was about to make a quick answer; after all, he'd been in bed with her a few times. Then he got to thinking about her more carefully. "Nobody knows that skirt," he allowed. "She's a smart one fer a woman. Hard too." He thought about it a little more and added, "She wouldn't stop at havin' either of us put away if we got out of line."

"That's what I figured," Mountain said. "I looked her over good when I was in St. John. She wasn't by some chance plannin' to have you and Schoolboy get rid of me after we pulled the job for her?"

Lobo hesitated. "She didn't mention it, an' that's a fact. I wouldn't put it past her, though. In fact, me an' Schoolboy wondered if she wasn't plannin' to cut us out."

Mountain winked. "How'd you feel about cuttin' her out?"

Lobo involuntarily snorted. "I reckon I kin trust you," he said. "Me an' Schoolboy was figurin' to put sich an idee up to you, as a matter of fact."

"Easy enough to do," Mountain said, gloating inwardly. "I had something like that in mind. It looked like you and Schoolboy might get in the way."

"Not us," Lobo said. "The less folks to cut in, the more we take. She was figurin' on takin' the big cut and doin' the least work."

"That's the way it looked to me and Harris," Mountain said, referring to his mate. "Here's what we figured. I'm fixin' to put in to St. John pretendin' I've got some repairs to make. No one'll get suspicious. I aim to tie up down along the bluff below town a day or so before they take the big haul out to the *Ira Baker*. I looked around down there. An old road runs from the road down to the dock. We can pull the heist in the brush between town and the dock, then run right down to the *Greyhound*. The whole thing'll take about five minutes. We can be gone before anybody gets organized."

"Yeah," Lobo said, "And Morgette'll be with the wagon and the safe. And maybe Hennessey, too. I sure as hell ain't gonna miss 'em at fifty feet."

Mountain laughed wickedly. "If you do, and I don't figure you will, I got about a half dozen boys'll be helpin' out—all of them with Winchesters."

CHAPTER 23

AS they prepared to haul the safe with most of the spring cleanup down to the *Ira Baker*, Dolf swung up onto the seat with the driver. Old John took ahold of his arm. "Don't be so all-fired anxious to leave," he said. "Nobody's gonna grab that box up here and run. Have another coffee and cigar. The boat ain't pullin' out till I git thar anyhow." He tipped a wink at Maggie, who was standing on the loading dock. "Besides, Maggie ain't in any hurry fer you to leave jist yet either. Are you, honey?"

She shook her head. She was never in a hurry to see Dolf go anywhere. In fact, if it hadn't been for the two children, her clinic and the school, she would have insisted on going with the men.

Therefore, only Rudy and Hubie were in the wagon with the safe, Rudy driving, as they headed from Old John's down toward the *Ira Baker*.

Neither was expecting trouble as they rounded the bend, briefly out of sight of both the trading post and the *Ira Baker*. The narrow road wound between muskeg bogs and willow brush. They were approaching the branch road that led down the river when, without warning, Lobo Lafferty stepped from the bushes. Rudy always carried a six-shooter as a matter of form and he had an extra one with him this morning, just in case.

"What the hell?" said Rudy, putting his hand on a six-shooter.

Hubie's heart was in his mouth. He'd always been more scared of Lobo than any of the others. Irrationally he thought, Nilda found out! She sent him! I'm gonna die! Me and Lizzie will never get back to that farm. . .

Lobo confidently grabbed the bridles of the horses. Then Schoolboy stepped out. Lobo had a rifle in a sling over his shoulder, plus a six-shooter stuck into his belt. Schoolboy had no guns in sight.

"Let go o' them hosses," Rudy said. "What the hell you tryin' to pull?"

A new voice entered the conversation. Hank Mountain stepped into the road with a leveled rifle. "We're tryin' to pull a stickup, yuh damn fool. What does it look like? Jist turn them hosses down this way and nobody'll get hurt."

Rudy debated pulling a six-shooter, but just then three of Mountain's crew stepped into sight, also with leveled rifles.

The sharp report of a small gun startled them all—even Hubie, who'd been responsible. He'd pulled the nickel-plated twenty-two with which he was a "crack shot," taking a desperate gamble to save his life and be around to take care of Beckie Brewster all her life. He did it as if he were in a dream, hardly believing that this was really happening. A hole appeared right where he'd aimed, between Lobo Lafferty's eyes. The big man collapsed in the road, dead.

This diversion gave Dwan a fair chance to jerk his .45 and take a snap shot at Mountain. He hurried too much, and missed. The horses leaped into their collars, lurching forward. Mountain grabbed them and turned them down the side road. Hubie had fallen out at the first lurch. Now Dwan leaped out as the wagon swayed on two wheels, to avoid possibly being pinned under it or the safe if the wagon overturned. Chased by several Winchester shots, he scrambled frantically for the brush. He dove behind a hummock and might have been safe if he hadn't wondered what had happened to Hubie. He bobbed up and took a look. Schoolboy was just about to brain Hubie with his slung shot. Hubie was helpless on his hands and knees—either dazed from his fall, or wounded. Rudy took deliberate aim and cut down Schoolboy. He waited till he was sure of his shot, then turned both six-shooters to spray anyone in sight. As he did he caught a Winchester slug in the thigh. It dropped him in the muskeg.

When Dolf and Old John reached the scene, followed shortly by Maggie, only Hubie was standing, slightly dazed, his dinky .22 still dangling from his hand. The horses and wagon were not in sight. But the bodies of Lobo and Schoolboy were clearly visible. Rudy's shot had cut through Schoolboy's rib cage, piercing his heart. A brief examination told them that both Lobo and Schoolboy were dead. Dolf and Old John soon found the team at the edge of the bluff above the river, the wagon spilling into the brush at the very brink of the cliff, prevented from going over only by the team.

"Damn safe musta dropped off inta the drink," Old John said. "We'll fish it out later. Let's get Rudy up to camp where Doc can work on that leg." They untangled the team and wagon and used it to transport Rudy and the bodies.

"I don't need that kind of company," Rudy complained.

Just then Doc showed up and told him, "Shut up while I put something on you to stop the blood." He improvised a tourniquet from his bandanna, tightening it with a stick broken off a nearby spruce.

Maggie had taken Hubie in charge. He had started to tremble, the full import of what he'd done just sinking in. "Sit down awhile," she told him. He flopped on his ample rear beside the road, white and breathing hard.

"I never felt like this," he said. "I never killed anybody either." The words came out unevenly, his jaw trembling as he spoke.

Maggie stroked his forehead. "You did just right," she assured him. "You'll be okay in a minute. It's just a little shock."

"There were at least four more robbers," Hubie said shakily, realizing that the others had all gathered around him.

"Where the hell'd they go?" Old John asked.

"I think down the road where the wagon went."

An impromptu posse headed by Dolf and Old John started that way. They followed the road a couple of hundred yards to the bend in the river, topping out on the bluff. The *Greyhound*, under full steam sending forth black smoke, was still in sight.

"Goddammit!" Old John roared. "I'll bet that bastard Mountain plucked the cleanup. I shoulda suspected." He watched with the experienced eye of a steamboat man. "Fast," he said. "If the safe's on that thing we'll never in hell catch 'em."

"I think the safe's down there in the river where the wagon got hung up," Dolf said. "They probably figured to get it down to the boat, but the fight Rudy and Hubie put up threw them off."

The safe wasn't under the bluff in the deep water. They tried to grapple for it, then built a rough coffer dam and dug for it, but they found nothing. This took several days. Meanwhile Dolf had gone to St. Michael on the *Ira Baker*, keeping a lookout for the *Greyhound*. It had beat them to St. Michael by several days and was abandoned there. No trace of Mountain or his crew was found once they departed for the outside on the *Portland*. A subsequent check of the Pacific Coast ports indicated that they'd passed through, but they'd apparently split up and vanished. None of them were ever found. The verdict was that the *Greyhound* robbers had somehow transferred the safe on board and made off with it.

"Damn if I see how," Old John said, "unless they slid it down some planks right from where the wagon was hung up in the brush. If they did they sure as hell moved like lightnin'. We was down there in less'n a minute to Hubie; and less'n another two or three minutes to where the hosses was."

And there the case rested. The only happy note was that the shipment had been fully insured. The boys sending out gold for families back home didn't have to face the bleak prospect of their families starving while they spent another year grubbing out a new stake.

Hubie and Lizzie had departed on the *Ira Baker* with Dolf. Hubie was certain it was the healthiest thing for him to do. He wondered how soon Nilda and her remaining goon, Shiv, would discover that there was no gold dust buried under Old John's trading post. He certainly didn't care as long as he and Lizzie were on their way to Nebraska.

It was early fall with the geese heading south when Old John discovered that his basement was all dug up. He didn't immediately connect this with the somewhat surprising fact that Nilda had tearfully parted from Doc and sold out the Skookum Too after only one season—and an obviously profitable one at that. In fact, it was when he found out that she'd also sold out in Juneau and evaporated with Shiv that he really began to think seriously about her.

"Do you suppose," he asked Dolf, "that Hubie might have pulled the wool over all our eyes and cleaned that safe out for Nilda before it got heisted? He *was* Goldie's brother, don't fergit. Why else would someone have been diggin' around down there? He could have run it down through the trap door any night with a little help. He had the combination to the box. They could have slipped it out in them beer cases. There was at least a thousand of 'em."

Dolf thought about that. "I don't think so. Dwan would have had to be in on it." (By now Rudy had also pulled out, ostensibly back to Montana.)

"So?"

Dolf mulled that over. "Well, I gotta admit that Rudy wasn't any angel. But why would him and Hubie have put up a fight if they knew the safe was empty?"

"Damfino."

"I think I can answer that in Hubie's case. He might have thought Nilda sent Lobo and Schoolboy to kill him for running off with Lizzie. He told me as much. That's why he jerked out that dinky and let fly. But I can't say about Rudy. I reckon he tried to save Hubie's life. He always had his good side."

"How do we account for Mountain's outfit then?"

Dolf said, "I'm bettin' they was workin' for Nilda. She used 'em as a red herring in the first place, and was shrewd enough to keep 'em around to copper her bet to get the gold—no matter *what* happened."

"Figurin' Rudy and Hubie might double-cross her?"

"Exactly. That is, if they were supposed to pipe it off."

"I can hardly see a gal plannin' all that out."

"She was probably just takin' over Goldie's scheme in the first place. Then she probably improved it a leetle. She was a lot smarter'n him—she could have planned it herself, I'd bet."

Old John just shrugged. There the speculation rested. Dolf figured they'd probably never know. It was only the next year, when Old John pulled up stakes himself, and decided to retire, that Dolf got to thinking about someone else who'd had the combination to the safe and could have drained it before it was toted out. Old John. The fast *Greyhound* was more like something he'd have done than either Goldie or Nilda. He'd been a riverboat man for years on both the Mississippi and Missouri. He and Mountain were old friends. Even if Goldie had had it built in the first place, Mountain might have tipped off Old John and suggested the two of them do it, first emptying the safe, then use the *Greyhound* to dispose of the evidence—the empty safe itself.

Old John's conduct was certainly something to think about. As far as Dolf knew he hadn't planned to leave Alaska for years. And it seemed a little strange that he'd pulled Dolf off the wagon at the last minute. It was what he'd have done to avert a fight and keep his friends from killing each other. John knew Dolf would have put up a fight, but had no reason to suspect that Hubie and Rudy would. Only Lobo's and

Schoolboy's being present was hard to explain if in fact it was Old John's deal. In that case, most likely, they were there representing Nilda, and neither Old John nor Mountain knew how to get rid of them ahead of time without arousing suspicion. However, either was capable of having them put out of the way later. Or had they been working for Old John all along?

EPILOGUE

For years, Maggie had heard all this mulled over in the Morgette family circle. Only now, when the safe had been found, had they finally learned what had happened to it. "Just think," she said to Dolf. "All those years it was sunk in the muck. It must have tipped out of the wagon when it swung down that branch road, and fallen in the mud. I wonder why we never thought of that?"

Henry said, "Well, Mom, we'll know soon enough about the big question—whether it was an inside job or not."

By then they were all back on the Morgette porch, the army contingent invited to coffee and rolls.

Henry looked at his father and said, "I know why you thought it might be an inside job, but if the safe is empty, who emptied it?"

Dolf set his cup down and took out a cigar, not answering immediately. After his cigar was lit, he said, "Well, son, like you said, we'll at least know *if*, even if we never know *who*, when you fellows get the safe open."

Maggie said, "You're not answering the question."

Dolf grinned. "I wouldn't put it past anyone who had the chance, even Old John."

That really surprised her.

Dolf described the aftermath of the robbery, explaining to the army people why they thought it might be an inside job.

Colonel Hancock was intrigued, as most people would have been. He said, "If the safe is empty maybe the stuff is still under that old building. Why don't you let us look? Whoever dug for it might have missed it."

Dolf hadn't thought of that. They'd lived right next to Old John's former trading post for years, and yet the idea had never occurred to them. "Go ahead," he offered, "if the safe is empty."

"What's your bet, Mr. Morgette?" Colonel Hancock asked.

"I ain't a bettin' man," Dolf said.

Not to be turned aside, Hancock asked Maggie, "What do you think, Mrs. Morgette?"

"Empty," Maggie said. She really had no idea why, but that idea just seemed more intriguing to her. "What do you think, Henry?" she asked their son.

"Full," he said. "How about you, Colonel Hancock?"

"Full."

Maggie looked at the two corporals. "We haven't given these boys a guess. What do you think?"

They both went along with her ("empty") probably because she'd been the only one democratic enough to let them in on the game, or perhaps because it was a golden opportunity to disagree with two colonels.

"We'll take it down to the shop and cut it open with a torch," Colonel Hancock said, getting up.

The men took it from the truck with a forklift and soon cut the hinges off with a blowtorch. It really hadn't been much of a safe, being more for appearance than real security. With the hinges cut it was short work prying the door off.

They all gathered around and looked.

Inside were rotted canvas bags from which gold dust poured out in small streams.

Dolf grinned. His instincts about Hubie and Rudy had been right.

"All this could be yours," Colonel Hancock told Dolf and Maggie. "We found it on your land; the army is only leasing it for the duration, you know."

"It was insured," Dolf said. "Probably belongs to some insurance company if they're still in business."

"Not necessarily," Colonel Hancock said. "I was involved in a case like this before. Lots of years have gone by."

Dolf shrugged. "Some court'll decide I reckon." To Maggie he said, "If we get it, we'll buy you a new dress."

"What's the matter with this one? It's only five years old."

In another half hour they were back on their porch. Dolf resumed his former position and again pulled down his Stetson. He said, "Derned if I'm gonna let a million dollars disturb my beauty rest any longer." In a few minutes he was snoring lightly, just as he had been before the army had interrupted him.

Maggie looked lovingly at him and wryly concluded, "Money mad."

It was one of the things she'd always loved best about him.

MORGETTE IN THE YUKON

G. G. BOYER

Dolf Morgette is determined to head west, as far west as a man can go—to the wilds of Alaska to join the great gold rush. He's charged with the responsibility of protecting Jack Quillen, the only man alive who can locate the vast goldfields of Lost Sky Pilot Fork. For Morgette, the assignment also holds the possibility of a new life for him and his pregnant wife, and perhaps a chance to settle a score with Rudy Dwan, a gunslinging fugitive working for the competition. But a new life doesn't come without risk. Morgette's journey has barely begun before he's ambushed. Soon he's beset at every turn by gunfighters, thieves and saboteurs. If he's not careful, Morgette may not have to worry about a new life—he may not survive his old one.

___4886-8 $3.99 US/$4.99 CAN

Dorchester Publishing Co., Inc.
P.O. Box 6640
Wayne, PA 19087-8640

Please add $2.50 for shipping and handling for the first book and $.75 for each book thereafter. NY, NYC, and PA residents, please add appropriate sales tax. No cash, stamps, or C.O.D.s. All orders shipped within 6 weeks via postal service book rate. Canadian orders require $2.50 extra postage and must be paid in U.S. dollars through a U.S. banking facility.

Name_____
Address_____
City_____ State _____ Zip_____
I have enclosed $ _____ in payment for the checked book(s).
Payment <u>must</u> accompany all orders. ❏ Please send a free catalog.
    CHECK OUT OUR WEBSITE! www.dorchesterpub.com